HOW

HOW

Geoff Wyss

 THE OHIO STATE UNIVERSITY PRESS | COLUMBUS

Library of Congress Cataloging-in-Publication Data
Wyss, Geoff.
 How / Geoff Wyss.
    p. cm.
 ISBN 978-0-8142-5183-6 (cloth : alk. paper)—ISBN 978-0-8142-9289-1 (cd)
 1. Short stories, American. I. Title.
 PS3623.Y747H69 2012
 813'.6—dc23

Cover design by James A. Baumann
Text design by Juliet Williams
Type set in Adobe Sabon
Printed by BookMobile

∞ The paper used in this publication meets the minimum requirements of the American National Standard for Information Sciences—Permanence of Paper for Printed Library Materials. ANSI Z39.48–1992.

9   8   7   6   5   4   3   2

CONTENTS

ACKNOWLEDGMENTS

Thanks to the following journals in which these stories first appeared: *Tin House*, "How to Be a Winner"; *Image*, "Child of God" and "Kids Make Their Own Houses," reprinted in *New Stories from the South* 2006 and 2009; *New Orleans Review*, "Exit Strategy"; *Gargoyle*, "Arms"; *Yemassee*; "How to Be a Better You"; *Painted Bride Quarterly*, "Profession of the Body"; *Northwest Review*, "Or"; *Puckerbrush Review*, "How I Come to Be Here at the GasFast"; and *Glimmer Train*, "Saints and Martyrs."

How to Be a Winner

THE FIRST THING IS, it takes guts. Let me hear you say it! Guts!

Men, when you have gotten to know me better, you will understand I am an individual who I am prepared to repeatedly demand or ask a question until I get my desired response. I am an individual who in my mind and heart there is constant focus on a goal. When you boys have locked up your pads and you're on your way home to Mommy or maybe you're quote kicking it with friends, I am a person who odds are almost a hundred percent I am still in my office devising a punishing, foolproof offense. I have in my office there's a coffee maker for late nights and film of you name the coverage or blocking scheme and I've got film of it, and this is me choosing to excel. Or sometimes, for health reasons and what have you, I drink green tea.

So my prerequisite question I'm asking is, are you able to look in the mirror and say this is a person with guts? Not am I a cruel person. Not am I unsportsmanlike in terms of hits to the knee or do I fall into the trap of performance-enhancing drugs, that whole spectrum. But am I a person who could fashion my own tourniquet in a war setting and return to battle? Am I a person who the Ten Commandments is my guiding code, which things like the Internet make it harder for you as young people than it was for me? Am I man enough to befriend a homosexual or a retarded individual despite I am a looked-up-to athlete, because everyone is deserving of respect? If you can say yes to these integrity benchmarks, my vow here today is that maybe you are five-foot-one like this gentleman in the front row, and maybe you have a, what is that, son, an eye patch? over your eye, but I will teach you how to be a winner.

So you are 0-5, 0-2 in district play. OK. Your coach has contacted me for the purpose of we're going to rectify that. My name is Cleveland Miller, and I am what is known as a sports behavior consultant, or simply a consultant. As a coach, my players referred to me as *Coach Killer* for the style of play I harped. I had a trademark of everyone in the state knew I was going to run the football and I ran the football anyway. In my last three years at Meequeepanassatommee High School, Storrs, Connecticut, my teams compiled a record of 36-1 and brought home two state titles. For the last four years, I have been an individual brought into various programs and et cetera, work environments and even governments, for mental toughness and success orientation. You may recall in your memory a period when Jay Cutler of the NFL Denver Broncos lost confidence in his mid-range game, specifically over the middle. This was widely reported. The person called in on that matter to restore Jay's way of thinking vis-à-vis throw with your eyes, not with your arm was me, and I induced him with anecdotes of let's look at how the greats did it and a visualization mini-retreat, which the next week he threw three touchdown passes. My moniker or what have you is I mix modern technology with old-fashioned I know what makes people tick. But I want to let you know that in your case today, I have waived my fee because I have watched the tapes your coach sent me and heard his cry from the wilderness. Men, be not afraid. Follow me. I have come to lead you forth.

Specifics of you're doing this wrong and you're doing that wrong we'll save for the field. But what the tapes are showing as a general sphere are missed tackles and confusion about where do I line up for the play in question, which these are mental or will-power mistakes. My notes indicate a recurring facet of it basically looks like you're handing the ball to the opposing team, which this is like giving candy to a girl who's already trying to kick you in the nuts. I saw individuals in this room trip and fall purposely to avoid physical contact. Then there are what you would call the football stupidity or a nicer word would be lack of knowledge issues. The offensive unit lined up on the wrong side of the ball not once this season but twice. That's five yards right there. I had to make a new category in Excel for plays you ran with only ten men on the field. Then, number three, there are the issues of lack of self-caring about yourself and your teammates. One particular individual whose number I won't state but whose position involves predominantly running the ball with stamina was captured for posterity lighting a cigarette under the bleachers and slowly enjoying the rich tobacco flavor. Let me guess that the reason I hear giggling in the back of the room is listen now and see if I've got it is because you have told yourself if we are going to lose anyway, then losing will not hurt as much if I put myself in a passive or female position, go ahead, other team, eff me and get it over with. See, here's the thing is, I have coached losers before. I know and sympathize the mentality. I have coached many losers successfully, and this is what qualifies me to aggress and incent you. At Meequeepanassatommee High School, Storrs, Connecticut, I took young men whose major yearn was huffing chemicals and self-touching themselves in the lavatory, and I turned them into *yes-ma'am, yes-sir* type of people who would have eaten my enemy's heart off a spear. Did I have my critics, so to say? Yes, I did. But a rule of life you can say Cleveland Miller taught you is your critics are people who secretly wish they could be you. They are frequently English teachers and Math teachers, and they sit on school boards and whisper-campaign about what they call abusive and coercive treatment. They are people who according to a tape measure may be the size of a full-size person, but they preside in your memory as approximately a midget. They never played the game, and they will never know the inner joy and feeling of hit or be hit. They notify their decisions to you on the letterhead of a law firm instead of we're going to speak to you face to face and fire you as a man. Son, look at me. Spit out that gum, look at me, and listen as I tell you the story of Michael Wiltonberry.

There are many types of loser. Michael Wiltonberry was the kind where the word I use for it is smug. This is a word that means clever combined with a sort of facial look that is begging authority figures to punch you in the mouth. I knew Michael as a student in my health class with leather wrist bracelets on his wrists and hair over his eyes, which that was his message he wanted to send and I got the message. His main hobby in class was writing offensive material on small pieces of paper, this would be female vaginas and jokes about my teaching approach, and passing them to other students. But all that changed the day I entered the student lavatory on what they call a whim and intercessed Michael handing a plastic bag of narcotics to a fellow student. If there is a national or international drug of people everywhere who have no goals, it is marijuana or weed, which was the contents of this bag, which I plucked into my keeping. But: did I see this incident as this is a bad or negative moment in life, no good can come of it? Something to get downhearted? No: because winners are never downhearted, this is a hallmark. Because fate may have given Michael Wiltonberry a father who only saw the sun when the law dragged him out into it, but it also gave him a six-foot-three frame with high physical I.Q. and surprising foot speed. I took the plastic bag like this, and I placed it in the toilet like so, and I applied the flushing mechanism. And I looked at Michael the same way I am looking at you, young man, as an individual of infinite potential. And I expressed my hope that he would show up for spring football practice the next morning with cleats and a hairstyle suitable to a young man of the male gender.

This seventeen-year-old boy had the lungs of a coal miner, but I addressed that situation by making him throw up his old lungs every day until he developed new ones. Experience had taught Michael he could remedy a cure for everything by crying, and I provided him a new experience where crying gave him more things to cry about. I saw Michael's car entering a McDonald's one night after practice, a cry-for-help mobile with heavy metal or maybe the lingo is goth markings, and I took him home so my wife could make him a proper supper. A sit-down meal is one of my messages to you, men. Plates you can't fold and forks made out of metal, you report to your parents regarding I learned this or that about the world today, what wisdom do you have for me, your loving son. My wife served I'll always remember it was pot roast that night, and Michael took seconds. His favorite dish in the long run was this baked chicken with my wife puts bread crumbs on it, which Michael came to my residence for every Monday night, Monday being the night his mother was pre-engaged committing adultery in various taverns. How anyone could become so wasteful with what God has given them, which you would think loving and caring for your child would be universal, this is the question I ask myself. My wife was unable to have children personally. There was a medical term we were given. But—but my point I'm trying to express to you young men here today is how I ran Michael at practice and fed him at home and dragged him out of parties by the neck to reverse-motivate his bad habits and, yes, a couple times at the beginning I let my players teach him lessons of respect in the locker room. And eventually the outside loser was washed away to reveal the inside winner of Michael James Wiltonberry. This was remarked by everyone who crossed his path, including his grades went up in his core subjects. And next fall he led my team to the state finals, where he played the last nine minutes of the fourth quarter with a torn ACL. So when I tell you this is a winner and that is a winner, and when I use a word like son in the context of that's how I saw Michael, you will understand certain things the school board did not, such as maybe there is a good reason a player would spend the night at a coach's house. Such as maybe human life doesn't always fit your rule book. So I had to leave that job. But I still speak to Michael by phone, and I want you to know that he excelled in Division II college football until he was reinjured and today is a grocery store manager or is on that track is what they call it, and he has two healthy children.

I sometimes consider that today's world possibly makes young people afraid to win. Whether there is something to that. That there is a sense of everything is dirty, everyone is lying. That there is a so-called hedonism of I have to always be enjoying myself. But, men, please understand, and there is no doubt in my mind or should be in yours about this: the world is broken down into half the world is winners and half the world is losers. We have what is known as a locked struggle. The losers are trying to make losers of us all. This is their armageddon goal, and they are constantly attaining toward this goal with persuasive this and attractive that, mostly things of the body. But if we winners surrender, the world can say good-bye to the following. The precision excellence of football. American military superiority. Inventions to improve the daily lives of people from caveman times to now. Trust among humans based on here is my word and handshake. And hello to the following. Constant sex jokes in films, suck you, suck me. Everyone is obese. Cities are you can't even go into them without a machine gun. And one day when we're all watching TV, Ayatollah Busybody gets elected President of the World. It's a locked struggle. The championship of the world is at stake. You can take the first step toward winning that championship when we go out onto the field today.

So grab your helmets, men. I am going to teach you speed concepts, and I am going to teach you pre-game. I have studied Buddhist meditation, and tomorrow I will insert that component. I asked you to spit out that gum, son. Only losers have to always be doing something with their mouths. That's the main organ of losers, their mouths. Ours is our guts, men. Say it with me! Guts!

Child of God

THERE IS NOTHING MORE DELICIOUS to teachers than a student getting pregnant.

The moralistic hand-wringing of the older teachers, whose lives have become a thin gruel; the knowing grins of the twenty-somethings, still racked by their own bottomless appetites; the general adult glee of watching carefree youth dragged into the confraternity of woe; the secret satisfaction all teachers feel when their admonitions, ignored, are made flesh: a student pregnancy offers something for every taste. Teachers are scavengers. We'll eat anything if it's free, and we're no more discriminating in the gossip we consume. Like the kids who make their lunch from the candy machine and know their diet is death, we gorge on the abundant, sugary whisperings of our high school, too overworked and too polluted to search out better fare. Given the way the pregnancy of our soon-to-be valedictorian appealed to our deepest gut, it was only fitting that we were discussing it at the lunch table.

"Bye-bye, college," sang Jason Pete, our assistant basketball coach. He listened to what he'd just said and giggled, blackly and helplessly, the way you might in response to the death of the last giant panda. "Bye-bye."

"Where'd she find the time, is what I want to know." This was David Bonvillian, the chemistry teacher, warming up his toothy smile. David got away with saying the things no one else could say because he said them in a voice so loud that everyone's internal censor ducked. "Yearbook. Cheerleading. Student Council. Fucking. There's got to be a daily planner involved."

Jason mimed the act of writing.

"*Monday: wake up and vomit. Tuesday: wake up and vomit.*"

"*Wednesday.*" David again. "*Observe softening and expansion of own pelvic bone. Physics quiz.*"

Jason and David enjoyed their usual chorus of tittering women, mostly first- and second-year teachers whose clothes were a little too nice. Claire LeBlanc, a counselor in her seventies for whom the body had exhausted its joys and who therefore thought the body an uncouth topic, stared at her Styrofoam lunch and chewed cheerlessly.

"The boyfriend's not even in school. Works at Winn Dixie," Jason said, a comment meant to indicate that Ashley Brimmer, our best student, an early admission to Emory, had opened her legs to the great average of our suburb, a shiftless, self-segregated exit ramp of economic helplessness, inarticulate rage, and bumper-sticker nationalism. That she had, in other words, made the choice so many of our smart girls had made over the years. I recognized in Jason's comment, and in David's response—*Maybe she did it to fulfill her service hours*—the jealousy of men who wished Ashley had, in some hypothetical universe where only men's minds can travel, chosen them instead, or pined away chastely for lack of having them. I was readying a statement that would triangulate our cynicism and heartbreak into something truer than either, a beacon we could navigate toward through this dark day, when Ted Infante entered the lounge.

Ted was the senior faculty member at Our Lady of Perpetual Succor, the Chair of Religion. A near-miss priest, he had married and raised a family and come to identify this most conventional of choices as saintly virtue. The most important lesson Christianity had taught Ted was smugness, and as moderator of the Student Ministers, he sowed this smugness through the religious life of the school. But the word *smug* suggests the confidence of special knowledge; Ted was smug the way the word sounds, like a creature hunched and snuffling in a cave, dumbly hugging a beloved totem tighter and tighter to its breast. Ted hated knowledge. You could track his ignorant path through the faculty lounge by the trail of crosses he drew with fine-point marker on every object he touched—his coffee cup, his briefcase, each new memo he pulled from his mailbox—to make it safe for use. Ted further defended himself against the actual with a stock of good-cheer phrases and an incessant mask-like smile, his eyes bunkered into slits. When you spoke to Ted, most of what you said, along with most of the evidence of the world, burnt up before it could pierce his outer atmosphere. But Ted didn't need global threats to feel embattled; he felt embattled, apparently, by the act of running copies, using the microwave, or taking a pee because he threw up a barricade of constant mumbling against all these activities, his voice rebounding off the proscenium of the urinal as he dandled his sanctified penis. His students and most of the younger teachers saw him as a harmless goof, cute and pettable, but I knew he was capable of making treacherous swipes with what he believed was a holy sword.

Jason and David fell silent when Ted entered, not because they feared his censure but because there was no way to involve him in the conversation that would not produce deep ennui; it would have been like playing pinball without the flippers. This left Ted to fill the vacuum with his dingbat buzzes and whistles: "All right, whew!" (Mopping his brow theatrically.) "We live to fight another day! It's halftime, ladies and gentlemen, halftime!" (Now squinching his nose to elevate his glasses and peer at people's lunch trays.) "OK, let's see what they're serving us here. Shepherd's pie. Heh, heh, question is, what's in the herd!" (A joke he had told a thousand times.) "That's the question. Never know! Never know!" and he drifted off toward the mailboxes like a car in traffic trailing music of surpassing stupidity.

"Wilkins," Jason said to me some moments later, "you're quiet today."

I felt my lips purse. I nodded, keeping my peace. Until Jason had spoken to me, I hadn't realized how tired I was. It's usually after lunch, when my resolve has gone soft as a pillow and all I want to do is lie down on it for a nap, that I wonder how the hell I'm going to do this for another twenty years, like Ted.

ON MY WAY to class, I dropped off some forms to Gilda, the assistant principal's secretary.

"Where would you like me to put these?" I asked.

"I'd tell you the truth," she said, "but I don't want to make you come in your pants."

"Who says I already haven't."

"Sick puppy," her leer turning feral. Gilda was the most profane person I knew, and I was very fond of her. She was a genius of naughtiness, patently smarter than most of the teachers, a woman who had given her intellectual energies not to science or history, but to her borderless marriage and its catalog of sexual languors, which she would recount upon request. Gilda could make a double entendre out of *anything*. For most people, sex toys were punch lines, never escaping the jokes they appeared in; for Gilda, they were everyday household tools which I knew she kept in a briefcase under her bed because she had told me the story of her grand-children discovering them. She liked me because I acknowledged her sexu-ality; because, being unmarried, I was not anchored to dutiful propriety like my colleagues; and because (championing libertinism in the abstract and sometimes enjoying its publications) I could keep up with her dirty talk. As for actual bad behavior, she was much better equipped for its rigors: three inches taller and eighty pounds heavier than I, she had the physical presence of a linebacker fortified by weaponized breasts and an audacious gush of platinum curls.

"You heard Ashley Brimmer's pregnant?" I asked.

"Ye-es," the word developing slowly, her eyes glinting, as if her secret society had secured the membership of an important and unlikely soul. I might have suspected Gilda herself of impregnating Ashley, if that were possible—and as Gilda bit her lip and bared her gums, I wasn't so sure it wasn't.

"You hated girls like that in high school, didn't you."

By *girls like that* I meant Student-Body-President, Cheerleading-Cap-tain, Homecoming-Queen, Treasurer-of-Student-Ministers girls—all the things Ashley Brimmer was.

"I did. But I loved their boyfriends. And their boyfriends loved me."

We stood enjoying the rich aftertaste of this joke in the windowless room where our lives had washed us up.

"At least she'll be able to finish out the year."

In the Archdiocese we hide our pregnant girls away at an alterna-tive school when they begin to show, but since it was already April, that wouldn't apply in Ashley's case.

"Well, they're discussing it this morning. Ted's pushing to get her out now."

My face compounded all the things it wanted to say into a pair of startled eyebrows.

Gilda shrugged.

"I just figure that, like every other man on campus, Ted's angry he wasn't the one who got to fuck her."

The bell interrupted whatever pithy summation I was going to make, and three minutes later I was teaching AP English with Ashley Brimmer in the front row.

We were wrapping up a quarter on the Greeks. Among the modern titles I had assigned was Forster's "The Road from Colonus," which ends with a tree falling and killing a Greek family of five in the very spot where an Englishman had wanted to spend the night.

"Fate works in mysterious ways," said Candice Monroe in answer to my question about theme. She had pulled one leg up underneath the plaid skirt our girls wear and wedged it at a youthfully impossible angle onto the seat. Hair exploded from her left temple in an insouciant brown spray. How wonderful it would be to be her, with her perfected teeth and her iPod full of silly music, her oversized ballpoint pen with its translucent cushioned grip and her sunny spot in the third row!

"God has a plan for all of us?" I paraphrased. "There's a cosmic purpose?"

"Yep."

I paused to give the others a chance to weigh in. These pauses—their length and weight, the questions I follow them with, the larger point I want to make about this story and all the stories I teach—were known to me from long experience, like lines in a one-man play of extended running, and in the quiet of my heart I considered Ashley Brimmer.

She sat in my foreground blur, in the desk right in front of me, clicking out and reinserting the lead of a mechanical pencil with the only part of her that was less than beautiful, her fingers. Those blighted nails were the first thing I'd noticed four years earlier, when she pointed to a question on my pre-test in English I. "Is this an introductory adverb clause?" she whispered when I knelt beside her desk. I reread the item; I had omitted a comma that changed the answer. "Oh, you're right. I'm sorry." I was about to stand and announce the change to the class when Ashley turned and whispered, "It's OK." At thirteen, a pretty girl's prettiness is transcendent. Ashley's skin and hair still carried the glow of their minting, untouched by time's trade and tarnish. Her body, all shoulders and elbows then, held itself light and straight in the desk, a posture that believed in everything except for evil and death. But it was her eyes that raised her beauty from a thing to an idea: they were so direct, so deeply black-brown, that I could barely muster the courage to meet them. Over the coming weeks, as she proved herself to be not only a magnitude brighter than the other students but also just as earnest as that first encounter foretold, Ashley's eyes and their expectations of me—that I be good and patient and self-sacrificing and honest—began to cast a radiant heat upon my cheek even when I was looking at other students. How many times in the last four years had I awoken to my morning alarm with Ashley's eyes staring from my preconscious, their blackness floating forward from the blackness of my room?

"Which character in the story makes a statement about fate similar to what Candice has just said?"

"Ethel." One of the boys in back.

"Where is it. Let's find the quote."

"Got it: 'Such a marvellous deliverance does make one believe in Providence.'"

So, Ashley's eyes. Ah, but those bitten fingers! She did so many things with them, from handstands at pep rallies to ticket collection at dances to playing piano at Mass, that there would have been no way for her to keep them nice anyway; but I finally caught her with them in her mouth. It was a changeover between classes during her junior year, the halls astream with students: I was standing in the doorway to my classroom pretending to be attentive to hallway conduct when I noticed Ashley gazing with complete stillness into the interior of her locker. She had lost track of the world, her eyes blind to the book she had begun to select with her left hand as her right unconsciously worked its digits one at a time into her mouth for a few tiny, complacent nibbles. It was one of the most tranquil and engrossing scenes I have ever witnessed, like watching a delicate bird groom itself on a silent ledge. When she finally snapped back to awareness and fluttered off down the hall, I remember thinking that the difference between voyeurism and sight is whether you mean to use what you have seen or to keep it safe inside you.

"And what sort of person is Ethel? What does Forster think of her?"

"She's just a daughter trying to look out for her father."

"Is she? Why does 'looking out' have to mean bullying him out of what he wants to do?"

"Well, where he wanted to stay is where the tree falls. It was fate that she made him leave."

Ashley's handwriting was as elegant and restrained as her general bearing. She wrote in slanted print, with pencil, and I had watched her lettering grow sleek and functional as it shed its girlish serifs and cinched its inefficient gaps. The word *Clytemnestra* upside down in Ashley's notebook was an architectural feat, a graceful unity of column and frieze. Where a girl in twenty-first-century America learns to practice grace, I have no idea, but grace characterized Ashley's handwriting and her posture and the motions of her thought, and I knew she was laying out of these sloppy early stages of the discussion the way a gifted high jumper waits patiently while lesser opponents grunt and mash their way through the lower altitudes and then overleaps them so simply and so without ego that they feel grateful to have witnessed their own defeat.

"Fate," she said finally, jamming the pencil behind her ear, a character-istic gesture, "is the same thing in this story as it is in the *Oresteia*—a word people throw around to justify their actions. The death of the Greek family has no meaning."

"So. Ethel's talk about Providence is just a way of putting a bit of fancy wrapping on her will. Like Antigone."

"Like Agamemnon. Like Clytemnestra. Like Orestes."

"Fate's a platitude for the shallow."

"And for the manipulative."

"Because what quote-quote purpose has the Englishman been saved for, do we find?"

"For complaining about the noise in his plumbing," she responded, smoothing the page with the flat of her hand. "Hardly a greater purpose."

"So Jocasta's right. Chance rules our lives, ignore everything but the now."

"No," Ashley said, enjoying the quaint trap I'd set as she nimbly side-stepped it. "That's the conclusion of O'Connor's Misfit. It's a false either/or, Mr. Wilkins." Neither of us had blinked in thirty seconds. "You told us that either/or is what makes tragedy."

My heart was a happy jumble. To have sown so diligently and to have the fruits of my labor returned so bountifully—I was overwhelmed by the beauty of the thing Ashley and I had made together, and I looked away in what could only be called embarrassment, even as Ashley's eyes fell shyly to her notebook.

Candice wanted very badly to be part of the fun.

"I think God knows what He's doing," she said with perfectly irrel-evant sweetness.

AFTER ASHLEY'S CLASS, fifth period, the rest of the day was a dullness and a drudge. I had two more sections of senior English, but they were non-Honors, which means that, far from a quickening of the mind that leaves the body receding to a vanishing point, I could look forward to repeating myself with heavy eyelids, performing broad, senseless gestures to compel attention, and using my face as a weapon of surveillance and deterrence. Every day of teaching involves at least one episode of conscious sweat-ing. It happens at cafeteria duty, with the humid chewing of five hundred mouths around you, or when your arm is lodged in the guts of an over-heated copier and you need double-sided quizzes for a class that starts in five minutes. This is the key to the unique exhaustion of teaching: the mind is called upon to do delicate work inside a constantly jostled container, like a painter made to paint inside a lurching public bus.

At the bell, I humped my twelve pounds of books through the shouldery mosh of the hallway to the locker of sophomore Nick Melville where, in a finely modulated light yell that only he could hear, I got him to admit that he had cheated on a test. Then, learning from a secretary that Doug Johansen, our assistant principal, had gone outside to watch football practice, I trekked across the blazing sward and, with the sun glinting directly into my brain, nudged the conversation with surgically cool disinterest until I learned that we had, indeed, decided to send Ashley away to the alternative school without delay, precisely because of her prominence on campus. Then I had to write a letter of recommendation for a surpassingly average student, a task requiring a mastery of faint adjectives and motionless verbs, a discipline much more demanding than actual praise, and I had to do so in a hard plastic chair produced in numbers too large for an attention to ergonomics and with a monitor whose blurriness I had to squint to correct in a building that had begun to slow-cook its contents now that the janitors had turned off the air conditioner. By the time I was licking the triplicate envelopes and signing across the seals, I could smell a uric, vaguely bookish reek coming off me. Then, at six o'clock, I sat down at my desk, shut my stinging eyes, and turned my mind to destroying Ted Infante once and for all.

It was, by now, the hour when people with families were putting chickens into ovens and huddling on couches, so I had the faculty lounge to myself. Ted's desk was as clean as his brain was cluttered, with only a radio, a crucifix, and a bonsai tree breaking up its broad expanse, and I navigated toward this queer trinity through the other twenty-some desks in the lounge. Scooting Ted's chair up behind me, I rubbed my hands together resolutely and slid open his top desk drawer. There was little of interest there, just some archaic office supplies, but I still experienced that brain-shimmer of trespass, that tinkle behind the eyes. He had a Pink Pearl eraser, its polygon edges scuffed a dull gray. He had an EZ-Grader with sliding sheath and brass corner rivets, and he had lickable ring-reinforcers. These were old-school supplies, relics from the age of paper, and they caused in me a feeling closer to pity than to detestation, so I shut them away from sight and began to rifle his file drawers.

Ted had penciled a tiny cross at the top of every document I pulled from its manila folder (worksheets on the patriarchs, flow-maps of the sacraments), a crawling black infestation of crosses. Even the folders themselves had been scribed with crosses, a tiny double-hatch on each tab alongside the description of its contents. Inspecting a test on Moses, however, I noted that it had a cross at the top of its first page only, leaving pages two and three unprotected from the wiles of Satan. And really, the bottom half of page one didn't look entirely safe to me, so far away from the citadel of the upper margin. A cross beside each question would have been a more responsible way to proceed—or, better yet, between each word. It might be prudent, ultimately, to replace each letter of each word with a cross to completely seal off all entry points for doubt and sin, though one would still need to consider a system for protecting each cross with a cross. . . . I shut the drawer and swiveled to the left.

The first file I pulled from this second drawer had no label, but halfway down its red flank, in Ted's penciled script, were the inevitable cross and the words, *Betrayals of Mission.*

The folder, which I laid atop the desk, was thick enough to call into service the widest pre-fold at its vertex; you could have written a nice fat title on its spine. I flipped the manila cover and read the first page, which had been produced on a manual typewriter:

August 30, 1971
INCIDENT: Assistant Principal Linda Lagarde was heard to remark that
            the current Pope was a political, not a religious, choice.
CONTEXT: Faculty Lounge, seven members of faculty present.

After *Context,* there followed a paragraph in which Ted cited the doctrine that had been violated and the way this violation undermined the religious mission of the school.

I didn't know the principal in question. She had left a decade before I arrived at Perpetual Succor. But a couple hundred more pages sat waiting beneath this first one, and I began to turn them: accounts of catechistic errors by Theology faculty, overheard doubts on the subject of transubstantiation, unsound discussions of Christ's humanity, the manually typed pages giving way in the 1980s to pages produced on electric typewriter and citing teachers I had worked with. I knew Ted well enough to guess he'd been funneling these accounts to the Archdiocese. I had the contents of the file spread rather haphazardly across the face of Ted's desk when the door from the copy room swung open.

Gilda took one step into the lounge with her armload of copies, pinned me with a sly glance, and said coyly, "What the fuck are you doing?"

She was wearing a red thing that on anyone else's body would have been called a *dress*, a garment of perfect respectability that Gilda's road-crew physique had somehow turned into a mockery of respectability, and you do not temporize with such a woman, so I said, "I'm digging through this motherfucker's shit. Come see."

I let her skim the top page to get the basic drift, and then I started thumbing the pages rapidly, looking for an *Incident* bearing my name. I didn't have to look far. Only two months into my first year at Perpetual Succor, Ted had slavered up to one of our Smith-Coronas and typed the following:

September 20, 1981

INCIDENT: *Teacher Gary Wilkins, while teaching Dante's* Inferno, *criticized the Church's stance on homosexuality by pointing out Dante's gentle treatment of homosexuals. "Homophobia is an Old Testament mindset. Jesus never condemned homosexuality. But most people, including the clergy, still aren't ready for the New Testament."*

CONTEXT: *I personally heard Mr. Wilkins's remarks as I stood outside his classroom. They were confirmed to me upon later questioning of his students.*

There followed a list of Bible verses and papal statements which my teaching had countermanded.

"He's nuts," Gilda said.

"He's not nuts. He's evil."

But I wasn't angry. This was one thing teaching had done for me in the years since Ted had first added me to his dossier: by buffeting me daily with a hundred annoyances and insults, with a hundred opportunities for anger, teaching had taught me to batten down my temper and navigate it calmly toward its intended port. At the beginning of my career, I was a person who screamed in traffic and gritted my teeth at student misconduct, a man with a legendary forehead vein; now, after twenty years, getting angry is something I do once, maybe twice a semester, and I do it slowly, with none of the old panic, loading my cannons and bringing my bow around so deliberately that my target is compelled to admit the justice of my volley.

So it was with a sense of amusement, really, that I thumbed forward from Ted's report on me to the point, several years later, when Bill McGee became our principal. It had taken Ted only ten days to find an error in Bill's behavior, some problem with a comment he had made after our first Mass of the year, and I lifted the remainder of the dossier out of its folder, some one hundred pages, and carried it to the copy machine.

"What are you doing, Wilkins?" Gilda asked in the slightly hushed tones of espionage as she followed me into the little room. I turned, reached under her shoulder, and pulled shut the door to the humid, humming oubliette.

"You know what McGee'll do to Ted for this kind of disloyalty? I'm getting the fucker fired."

Gilda leaned back against the table in the corner. "It's all so male and exciting," she said, perfuming her voice with the same slutty musk she used for sentences like *Why don't I ever get abducted?*, a parody of passivity as eerie as a wolf in your grandmother's sleeping bonnet. When I turned from the machine, having loaded the document handler, her eyes wore a challenging dreamy stare. "The way y'all are fighting over that little girl."

That little girl was obviously Ashley Brimmer, and while I didn't think Gilda's remark spoke to the truth of my actions, I knew that defending oneself against Gilda's sexual charges was like arguing with the Inquisition, it was easier to just admit guilt when the result was foreknown, so I turned and propped one foot manfully on a chair as the machine began to bump out its copies, and I said, "Can you smell the testosterone?"

"Smells like toner."

Ordinarily, I would have bandied the joke back at her—*It's pronounced BONER*, something like that—and the volatility of the moment would have dissipated into the enervated sniggers and sighs of the modern workplace. But I thought I detected a vague insult in Gilda's words, as if my life appeared dry and papery to women of full sexuality, as if I were not entirely real to them; and so, because I yearned deeply to enter that reality, and because I could think of no other way to do so than to blunder crudely forward, I took Gilda's hand, turned it palm upward, and cupped it between my legs.

"Does it feel like toner?"

I was swelling in her hand before she could unclasp my belt, which she began to do without looking down, smiling complacently as she dropped the buckle aside, twisted the tortoiseshell button beneath, and burrowed her hand warmly inside my boxer shorts. She was pressing me against her breasts and waiting for me to fill her encompassing grasp when the door clicked open and Ted Infante's head and shoulders spilled into the room.

"Oh, *hi,* Mr. Wilkins! Just dropping in to make some late copies. Teacher's work is never finished! Isn't that the truth, by golly. Being busy's a blessing, I guess!"

Gilda and I were too deeply entangled to do anything but stand frozen. Ted was so short to begin with, and the almost horizontal bow he was performing through the doorway made him so much shorter, that his head was perfectly on level with the offending activity; he was speaking, in effect, directly to my penis. Yet, astoundingly, he saw nothing. Perhaps his optic centers registered a calming uniform gray; perhaps the dominions and powers of angels had arrayed themselves in glowing tableau betwixt his eyes and the occasion of sin. His face took on a sort of glaze as he backed out of the room slowly and clicked the door shut, sparging words in his wake: "No hurry, no hurry. Take your time! I'll be in the computer room—computer's our real boss! Just holler, no hurry."

"Jesus Christ," I said a moment later, still pressed up against Gilda in a way that no longer seemed wholly appropriate. "Maybe he is nuts."

"Well, he's not an aphrodisiac," she observed, releasing the wilted item in her hand. "Some other time?"

I took Ted's originals back into the lounge and re-filed them in his desk. I put the copies in my own desk, and that's where they are still, in an unlabeled folder, supporting the illusion that I will one day use them. There is so much in my desk that's defunct: old tests based on grammar books we haven't used in ten years; student essays of note that I've never re-read and never shared with my classes; old student-body telephone directories, most of the numbers now obsolete; letters of recommendation I wrote for people who now own their own law practices or perform neurosurgery or who have had four kids in seven years and will never return to college. I must have once perceived in these materials a potential energy. But energy leaks, sighing away into the air, and time replaces the life of every object with a memory of its life.

Ashley Brimmer came to my classroom at lunch the next day to tell me she was being removed from school.

"I don't want you to be disappointed in me," she said, her voice cracking.

"I'm not. How could you think that?"

"I'm disappointed in myself."

"Well," I said, looking into eyes that pleaded for me to say something important, "that's a feeling you get used to as you get older."

"Are you disappointed in yourself?"

The way she asked this question, with slight emphases on *you* and *yourself*, revealed that Ashley saw me, remarkably, as someone who had risen above the conventional adult mire of compromise, regret, and despair. The shame I felt at having playacted my way into her esteem was surpassed only by the obligation to say something that would not further injure her.

"No. And you shouldn't be either. Go to confession or whatever, and then let it go. Leave guilt to the weak and stupid. They need it more than you do."

She smiled.

"Will you keep the baby?" I asked.

"Adoption."

We stood up from our desks and embraced, and she disappeared to the alternative school. But as I made my way back to the faculty lounge through an administrative back-hall of framed accreditation certificates and self-awarded plaques, the mendacity of my total being would not stop squeezing at my heart, and I was too tired to throw off its grip. My chest tightened as I walked, wringing loose a mist that rose and condensed in my eyes. I blinked at the moisture, but there was such relief in the blink that I could not bring myself to open my eyes again, there was nothing in that familiar hallway I could bear to look at, and I drifted forward through the lidded dark, leaving the known further behind with every step. Somewhere ahead there were secretarial desks, a potted tree, jagged file cabinets, but the darkness was too welcoming. Soon enough I would blow off course and end in wrack and ruin, but I understood that this was no more than the end I had been charting for myself all along.

Exit Strategy

EVERY TIME she used a kitchen knife, she imagined cutting her finger off. You know how your brain gets stuck, looping its junk on cue? Freaking itself out, filling time as it falls apart? Except that lately she'd been seeing it so vividly that she'd started to think it wasn't dementia, her mind misfiring, but a premonition: the knife slipping off a tomato and diving into the first knuckle of her finger, shushing through the bone, clean and for a moment painless, the exposed rings of her finger glowing like a lit cigarette. She had never cut herself in the kitchen. Didn't that make it more likely every time?

"Well, I think you're safe with that."

That was the plastic knife they had given her with her bagel, and the voice telling her this was the guy from the gym with the legs.

"Unless I frustrate myself to death with it."

"They make those all wrong," he commiserated, lacing his hands over one knee and watching her skim and re-skim the too-thin tip of the knife through the little cup of cream cheese, each time coming away with almost nothing. It was the kind of annoyance that might have nudged her into a whole day of hating contemporary life and her place in it if there hadn't been someone else there to turn it into comedy.

"How the hell do you make a knife wrong?"

"Maybe the Army Corps designed it," he said with a droll incline of his head that showed he kept this joke at the ready.

It turned out his name was Clay, which was perfect for a man who

owned an autobody shop and had a gearhead mop of orange curls lapping
over the collar of his polo shirt. She'd been seeing him at the Tulane gym
for years, where he had earned a place in the roster of half-humans she
knew by quirk and idiocy, by indiscretion and the private nicknames she'd
assigned them. Always wearing the same red running shorts, the kind
with panels that met in a high slit and advertised the flank of his ass, Clay
would thud about the gym on his fantastically thick shaven legs, and she
would glance from the TV attached to her elliptical trainer and think, *I'd
suck his dick* or some other similarly unprotected thought before flipping
to the World Series of Poker on ESPN2 because at least it wasn't Dr. Phil,
and then flipping back to Dr. Phil because her hate for him was so familiar
and bracing. Most men at the gym worked only their arms and chests,
the parts of themselves they imagined winning fights with, but Clay's
upper body was undistinguished, a little slushy, and he paraded his legs
among the apparatuses with a self-mocking joviality that seemed to say,
It's what I've got, let's enjoy it together! Which was mostly what he did
there, socialize, gabbing from victim to victim while Shannon scrupulously
avoided eye contact.

He was wearing those same red shorts this morning in the coffee shop
where, seeing all the tables taken, he had asked to share hers with an
inquisitive finger-pistol and a pow of his thumb that suggested she was
likewise part of his psychic landscape. And then, because he had offered
his name and occupation and how many people he employed and his belief
that small business would bring the city back and how nothing could ever
make him leave New Orleans in a million years—and because she had to
back him off with *something*—she had spilled across the table a gush of
caffeinated blather on the theme of self-mutilation. It was 7:00 A.M.

"It's so fucked up." She held the knife up, a pea of cream cheese at its
tip.

"Turn it upside down."

"Oh. That is better." She pointed at half her bagel. "You . . . ?"

"No, thanks. I don't eat breakfast."

"You know what they say."

"I do." He brightened at this first tip of the conversation in his direction. "About a lot of things."

The wry nod she gave, and which she was still dorkishly giving thirty
seconds later, might have looked to an observer like nervousness. But at
thirty-six she was post-nervous about men, just as she was post-voting,
post-screaming in traffic, post-really bothering with her hair, and post-

believing that her education had improved her in any important way. But making room for Clay in the three dimensions of her mind was doing a temporary violence to the disposition of all the other items there, and her words felt pushed to the side, looking back at where they used to be.

"So what do you think about Iraq?" He pointed at her *Times-Picayune*, where there was a photo of something bombed and sandy.

"You must be joking."

"My son's there."

"Your son? How old are you?"

"Forty-three. The math works out."

"Sheesh."

"I think we need an exit strategy."

"I think we need a we-shouldn't-have-fucking-gone-there-in-the-first-place strategy."

He backed his chair out.

"You want anything?"

"You drank that already?"

"I need like three or four of these to get going."

I'd say you're going already, she murmured as he powered off through the noise. In this context his legs weren't so daunting, less forged showpieces than everyday tools that would soon take him, like her, to work. She pictured him squinting through goggles at the sparking wheel of a disc sander, wielding multifarious forms of the word *fuck* in an atmosphere of clangs and hisses. His slicked legs and hard-rock hair were the parts of him he kept polished against the machine world whose cuts and scrapes owned his hands and whose junk lunches had colonized his midsection. So, strangely, just when he was farthest away—up handing his refill cup over the glass counter—he seemed to be standing too close, his details leaning into her personal space, and she slipped the rest of her bagel into the trash so she could dart when he returned. She had a hand on her purse and was standing when he swiped a business card to the table where her plate had been.

"There's a thing this weekend at my camp." His last name was DeLille, its letters in computer-cursive beneath a cartoon hot rod with swollen tires. "Barbecuey-type stuff, hanging out by the water. Just low key? If you're not busy?"

His mouth and eyes didn't seem to be doing any of the things she remembered men's mouths and eyes doing when they wanted to fuck you. And the card wasn't saying: it just lay there exerting its mute social weight, its doom of entanglements or evasions. But it would have been even more awkward for her not to take it than it had been for him to offer it, so she doffed the card at him and said she'd check her calendar.

"I didn't catch your name?" he said as she turned.

"Oh. Right. Shannon. Sorry."

Stuck, she crossed her arms in a narrow self-hug that didn't hide her six-foot frame any better than it had in tenth grade.

"You're Braid Girl," he offered.

"No shit," she said, equal parts pleased by the epithet and distressed at the intimacy of declaring and disarming their nicknames. "You're Leggy Joe."

Clay pursed his lips, admitting that he'd been pegged and that he loved it.

"Want to get capes?" He sparred the air. "Fight crime?"

"There's no crime in New Orleans. Just black-on-black whatever."

He shook his head, missing her irony. He wore an unfocused frown.

"I just don't get that. It's so sad."

DID CONVERSATIONS play and replay in other people's heads the way they did in hers? Echoing and recombining as she stood by the copy machine or took an extra minute in the restroom, just sitting in peace? Did other people find the insignificant so significant and the significant so meaningless? Did her employer have any idea how little of her active mind was required to do her job?

The braids she wore at the gym were purely utilitarian, keeping the long hair that serious women her age had long ago cut out of the sweat and stick. Except not really, because then why wear two? She made the braids quickly, without a mirror, and she wanted credit for their haphazardness. But she also wanted whatever credit might accrue to the braids as a conscious choice, stating something about her difference and inscrutability, the personal angle she took, and she spent a psychologically suspicious amount of time at the gym enjoying her ownership of the mystery she must represent to others as a grown woman with the braids of a child doing sit-ups on a resist-a-ball. Because the thing about the gym was, you carried yourself on a split screen to keep track of what everyone else was seeing as they assessed you in your every detail.

But work kept her late, and she skipped the gym. Her job involved performing the tasks of the twenty-first century in a position that interfaced

with positions all starting with the word *Assistant* and which was therefore difficult to define, a job that left the afternoon feeling about the same
whether she got home at four or six. No one surveilled her emails.

She fired one off to her friend Jill, who sat in front of her own computer across town, advancing the fiction that Clay, not a spreadsheet, had
nixed her workout.

How could he hold her gym-life hostage like that? That's what
it amounted to, because if she didn't go to his party, which she had no
intention of doing, she would either have to banish herself to the pool to
avoid him or lie to him in the weight room, and she always squinted when
she lied, people saw it immediately, and the tic got worse the longer she
rehearsed for the moment. And if she did go to his party, there would be
that trapped feeling you always get when food is prepared over fire? All
those hours while the fucking meat got brushed? Multiplied by twenty
people she didn't know and didn't want to, the product of which would
inevitably be drinking too much? You wave flies off the potato salad and
listen to some guy in a tank top talk about landing bull reds. You long-
suffer those silences when everyone just sits back and pretends to enjoy
nature. You know how every workplace has that freak who's always asking about your weekend and telling you you look nice and you have to say
fake stuff in return? That was Clay. That relentless niceness: what was the
pathology of that?

But in the end the word itself, *camp,* convinced her to go, because if
she didn't, she would end up watching *Saturday Night Live* with its noisy
syllable bumping through her head, reprimanding her about the kind of
fun people were supposed to have.

"Oh, it's like a party house," Jill chirruped. Jill had moved to New
Orleans only six months ago and was still stunned and cowed by the city,
by its words and weather, its advanced orders of beauty and terror. She
had apparently been expecting a tent and picnic table, men on all fours
blowing on tinder; instead, a dozen people lounged on cast-off couches
under the stilts of a raised house, a big-screen TV flashing in one open
corner.

Shannon pointed along the graying gravel road. "Check it out. The
next four or five were completely washed away. I bet he built this brand-
new since the storm." The lit windows above them were in fact still deca-
led by manufacturers' stickers. "What do people spend their extra money
on in Kansas City?"

"Just like. An extra car."

They weren't the sort of women who usually got attention at parties—
Jill was drawn with a straightedge and vagued in with watercolors and
wore glasses that looked twenty years out of date even though she'd just
gotten them last month—but Clay's friends didn't seem too concerned with
the usual. In a way that wouldn't have been acceptable in a world that
took itself seriously, a tiny, nervous man named Noah made straight for
Shannon and smoked at her in a manner so fiendish, his eyes birding to all
points of the compass, that his cigarette was revealed as merely a stopgap
between joints. Speaking to Jill directly made her splotch and cringe, and
this irresistible effect was soon being tweaked by Scott, a thickly furred
and deeply bellied man who could barely get his cigarette smoke jetted
from the corner of his mouth before Jill's latest one-word answer toed the
ball back into his conversational court.

"So you want to get high?" Noah asked.

They walked over among the sheared pilings of the next camp and
performed the rituals that, after a certain age, were performed in silence,
without ceremony or fanfare.

After the joint, Shannon considered getting back to protect Jill from
some of the torment the world was always causing her, but after all it
wouldn't hurt her to play grown-up for a while, and Shannon couldn't
really abandon Noah, who was rushing a cigarette alight and winding
himself up to speak.

"So are you and Clay . . . ?"

"No, we just met. Anyway, no. He's just a guy I know from the gym."

Noah had heard the one word that was important.

"Maybe we could go out sometime."

"I'm big enough to bounce you on my knee."

"I don't mind."

His voice was full of squeezed bravado, like a kid talking tough before
he cries.

"You like getting spanked and all that? Are you one of those guys?"

He shrugged, his throat making a noise of possibility, ready to consider
whatever shelter she was building against the world. Jesus, to wear your
need so nakedly!

"You like feet? Sucking on toes and all that?"

"Nnnn," he grimaced skeptically, then laughed a catch-up laugh when
he realized she was messing with him. "I don't think so."

"You've seen those websites?"

"Surfing. But I'm always like, why am I wasting my time on this when there are sites completely devoted to great big titties?"

"I'm at work this time, right. I forget what I was searching, but suddenly I'm looking at this guy with like shit all over his face. That was the whole thing, they would walk through garbage or whatever and then step on guys' faces."

"That's OK," Noah said, waiving his right to know about this particular byway in the labyrinth of human conduct. She realized that he was not so much squinting as marshaling all his energy to keep his eyes from falling the rest of the way shut. "Ever feel like you've seen too much?"

"Yeah, that."

"Yeah, that! Exactly!" Years of smoking had clipped a playing card across the spokes of his laugh.

"What do you do, Noah?"

"I'm a substance abuse counselor."

"Of course."

"Of course!"

So they were all partial people, people-fragments tumbling through the evening, until Clay, finished grilling, swept in to give them gravity and a centered system. The way babies enjoy the undisputed right to stun and occupy a roomful of people? How the phenomenon of a baby, its excellent oneness and how it hasn't fucked anything up yet, makes everyone forget the holding pattern of their own lives? That's what it was like when Clay bustled in, wiping his brow with a towel, and yanked a beer from the cooler, those smiles of dumb reverence all around. Scott whispered some bit of hagiography to Jill as Clay mussed the hair of a passing toddler. Three women who'd been sitting by the TV (one of them, Noah whispered, Clay's ex-wife) groupied up to ask about the best way to Hattiesburg and nodded as Clay sent a finger out from the neck of his beer to trace I-10 to 59 in the air. And then Clay was zipping in to land a peck on Shannon's cheek. "Look at you, you look great!" He followed this patent lie by drying his beer-hand on the bottom of his Saints T-shirt and snatching up Jill's skelly mitt, speaking his name into the daze of her face. "Don't let this guy feed you a bunch of lies," he warned, backhanding Scott's gut. "He's moving to Houston next week. Oh, hey, Shannon, Scott's a swimmer too!" pointing back and forth between them. In another age Scott would have been a pirate gnarling out tales of whiskered mischief, but in 2008 he was a male nurse, and his most swashbuckling feat was a third place in the

200 I.M. at the 1985 State tournament. Clay grinned at details he'd been hearing since high school and then somehow got Jill calmed down and talking about herself; and when Scott learned that Jill administered the intranet at Touro Hospital, he revealed the normal voice beneath the growl he'd been baying her with. Even when Shannon said one of those things she didn't know she was going to say and didn't really mean—*Fuck the Saints!*—Clay rolled his eyes left and right in jocular horror, unruffled and savoring life, the way you might at a child who blurts *I'm bored* during Mass. He was a freak of ease and charisma, a man fitted so perfectly to the shapes of the world that they felt like his own skin and voice. But did he know any one person, really? Wasn't unceasing charm just a way to keep everyone at the same distance? He seemed terribly genuine, but what was he—genuinely *what*?

She went upstairs to pee, moving herself beyond the party in mind and body, and sat considering the superior rightness of the shape of her own toilet seat. But between the bathroom and the steps back down, there was a blue couch that really wanted her to try it and whose cool suede spoke with all the persuasiveness it had gathered from the air conditioner about the idea of slipping off her shoes and putting her legs up, and then she was being awakened by a gray cat smelling her eyelid.

"That's Reggie," Clay said from somewhere behind her. Reggie arched against the hand she offered and then cantered off to his next appointment with a businesslike air. "He showed up after the storm."

"Who feeds him?"

She sat up to see Clay running water over a begrimed platter in the sink. Her head felt shrunken and set on a shelf, all its moisture leached.

"I'm out here every two or three days. Which if you ever want to just get away, let me know, I'll give you the key."

"Wow, OK."

"Oh," ineffectually snapping his wet fingers, "this Saturday? We're doing a fishing-tubing-drinking thing, a going-away for Scott. Jill's coming."

"She said that because she doesn't know how to say no."

It was excruciating! She stood up so she could better defend herself against his next solicitude, squinting to concentrate.

"That's my son," he said, thinking she was looking at a picture on the counter that she was in fact staring through. Inside the tilted plastic a boy willed himself faceless under a wedge of cap. "I need more pictures in here, don't I? I mean on the walls?"

"I'm so tired I can't really think about what you're saying." She managed two steps toward the door. "I was talking to Noah, and I somehow got stoned."

"He has that effect. You OK to drive?"

"Jill drove."

"Because I'm going that way, I could run you home and then bring you back out to the car tomorrow." Whatever it was you called the stuff that went on beneath a conversation, Clay simply didn't have much sense of it. But something in him had felt the dismal lean inside her and was trying to prop it back up with a double dose of cheer.

"She's a great kid, by the way. I'm really glad you brought her."

"She's twenty-six, so there's that whole thing."

"But super sweet."

"Whatever that means."

Finished at the sink, he crossed his arms and pretended to think about the nothing thing she had just said. Shannon was exactly torn between seeing what else he would agree with and getting the fuck out of there, except that getting the fuck out of there sounded infinitely better. Three quick steps would do it, but he would not stop nuzzling the bone of his idea.

"Anyway, I like her a lot."

That was one of those words, *like*, that if you said it a few times, didn't seem to mean anything. It sounded ugly, basically a turned-around version of *kill*.

"But who don't you like?" she asked. His eyes flinched in incomprehension. "I mean, you'd make friends with Osama bin Laden."

"I guess I never thought about it," finally beaten back. She said Saturday was iffy and got out before he could round the counter and give her another kiss.

SHE WAS A more generous person in the pool. Removing her contacts fuzzed all the handholds for her hate, and her senses swam to the center of their own soft ether. If Clay said he had *never thought about it*, maybe he hadn't, maybe for him there were only people he liked and people he hadn't met yet. Maybe that wasn't a mental illness. Maybe it took the Clays of the world to move people past their nicknames and make them human. She was human and should appreciate his efforts, respond to them. Because if you were a person whose way it was to run from people, that was life-denying, wasn't it? What do you think, you're better than life? Above life? You think you won't die at the end if you don't take part?

For five laps, she mummed along to Blondie's "Rapture" tinning from the poolside radio, her thoughts watering forth pictures—Noah blowing smoke at her tits, Jill's timorous shoulders, Reggie's face in convex—that floated dumb amidst the blue.

This was the only place she achieved grace. On land she hunched and clomped. She bumped into way more things than the average person. But in the water there was no hard or sharp, and the body could live its wish that the rest of the world were so, and the mind leaked into the body, wearing its buoyancy. Water diffused what land compacted.

Had she really asked Noah if he liked to be spanked? That was inappropriate, embarrassing. It was a way of talking scavenged from the trash of popular culture, and in this way it was typical of all her speech, which rooted through garbage while her better self averted its eyes. What her language knew best was its own dirt, so when a man asked her earnestly for a date, she mocked and titillated him with references to a perversion which itself she mocked without right or authority. This was the speech of a coward. The great crime of modern life was that it frightened people into banter. If she could speak always from the pool's undistracted blue, its underwater world-muffle, she would never need recourse to a word like *spank*.

How much did that undergraduate lifeguard weigh, one fifty? And what did she weigh, one eighty-five? Was there any way he could swim her up from the bottom if she sank there inert and lungless, her skin going dull?

People who prayed reported going forth into the day refreshed and fortified and certain of some center in the self. Swimming was the closest thing she had to that. But she couldn't make the peace she found there work outside the building, as if the god of Tulane's pool were a purely local deity, resident only in its trapped waters.

"HE BUMPED my boob."

"And then asked you out. After feeling you up."

"I mean, not my boob. We had on life jackets. But kind of. We both reached for a volleyball."

"Cute. Do you not realize that he is high ALL THE TIME?"

Because Jill was equally shaken by every tremor of existence, she had no sense of what was truly shocking, and she answered Shannon's question with the same apologetic but undeterred *No* she would have used to answer whether she knew who had won the last Super Bowl. She was wearing some kind of perfume for teenagers that Shannon could smell even over the three kinds of salsa the waiter had brought.

"Well, so, what. Besides Noah punching your tit and then beating off underwater, you just floated around in the lake and drank beer?"

"Scott almost drowned."

"He competed for a fucking state championship in swimming."

Jill's throat choked off one of its pained giggles, her eyes dropping with embarrassed affection for the memory.

"He jumped off the boat into an inner tube. It flipped upside down, and his feet got stuck in the air. Clay had to jump in and save him."

"Of course he did. Because he's Captain Ameri-Jesus. He's going to save us all." The image of Clay bounding from a pontoon boat made Shannon wonder what his legs looked like in swimming trunks, but not very much.

"He asked why you didn't come."

"And you said."

"That . . . you're a private person. Or something."

"'Cause, yeah. This looks really private, me and you in a public restaurant." It wasn't so much that Shannon had a history of estranging her friends as that her friends had a history of proving they were strange. "I mean, that's awesome. I don't come dumbass around with Moe, Larry, and Curly, so I'm a private person."

"Why don't you like him?" Jill rounded her hair tightly over one ear. "What's wrong with him?"

"If you don't know, I'm not going to tell you."

"Well, I don't know."

Jill made conversation like a bird, her head considering and reconsidering and never quite looking at the person she was talking to, her expression always some variation on worry, and it occurred to Shannon that maybe Jill's fluttery mien was less assigned by nature than assumed for personal advantage, even if that advantage was as pitiable as pretending to be dumber than she was.

"All right. You mean besides being boring?" Shannon saw the blossoming of Jill's delicate surprise and crushed it. "Because he's deeply fucking boring."

"Boring?"

"He's like one of those stuffed animals, you pull a string and he's all, *Let's be friends. Hey, I like you.* I don't see the appeal."

Jill shrugged again, this time defeatedly, as if a toy had been bullied from her hands.

"He's nice. He's really nice to me."

"For all you know. But three guys we just met, and you're out there alone with them on a boat? You're lucky you weren't gang-raped and thrown in the lake."

Jill's eyes aimed their distress in three or four directions, the last one Shannon's.

"Why would you say that?"

"Just—forget it," because the answers were too obvious to state. But as many times as she replayed Jill's question later, she couldn't get any answer to sound quite right, not to this or to any of the other questions crowding into the echo box of her mind.

ON SATURDAY she followed Clay home from the gym either to tell him his friendship was smothering and unwelcome, or to sleep with him and tell him his friendship was smothering and unwelcome.

He had made her half hour on the StairMaster a crawling torture, glomming over every few minutes and having to repeat everything he said because she had her earphones in the first time. Worse, he made her captive to the woman on the next machine, Crazy Jane, whom Shannon had long detested for the way she heaved herself retardedly against the stairs' resistance and grunted aloud to her iPod. Bad enough that he introduced them—Jane's sweaty, freckled hand shot out inescapably, her eyes leprechauning madly—but then he left Shannon alone to withstand a fifteen-minute nutmercial for Dennis Kucinich, the only benefit of which was that it made her feel better about not having bothered to learn anything about Dennis Kucinich. So when Clay said there was *this thing he needed her help with* at home, she shut down the machine in mid-stride and left Jane quacking happily to no one about a national reinvigoration of hope.

She left her braids in because if they were going to screw, Clay would probably want to think of her the way he saw her at the gym; but when they got to his house, he led her into a half-renovated bathroom and asked her to hold a faucet on center while he tightened some sort of nut from below. Rolling up and swiping dust bunnies off his ass, he appraised the finished work.

"Nice."

"That's what you asked me over for?"

Clay's whole face yearned to tell the truth and say yes. She watched it search for other philosophies of asking people over.

"I also need some help with this other thing."

"The faucet does look good," she said as he clashed his wrenches up off the floor.

"Yeah!" he brightened. "I got it from this guy."

"You're keeping the tub?"

"It needs new feet, but yeah."

"It's supposed to be good for resale."

How remarkable that life could still bring people to a moment when they had no idea what would happen next! The bathroom held itself with that particular afternoon stillness.

"So the grand tour," thumbing them into the hallway. "I just finished the room where the roof came off."

Now that she was only waiting for the right moment to make her final escape, feeling her freedom in advance, she was able to enjoy Clay's cloying geniality as he gave her the name of his crown-molding guy, explained how sponge-painting worked and offered to come do it for her, and then handed her a knife and onion in the kitchen, pretending he needed her help to make enchiladas. They sang "Mother-in-Law" with the radio, and Clay told her about the time he saw K-Doe in a fur coat piloting a rusty VW Beetle up Oak Street. Shannon had gone to K-Doe's wake at Gallier Hall, and Clay lapped up the details wide-eyed. But soon he was asking questions about her family and her future in the city that felt more intimate than any part of his body could have, so when he said, "What is this, Saturday? This could be enchilada night for us," she laid the knife down in mid-onion and said, "OK, so listen, Clay."

But her declaration was interrupted by the doorbell and three firm knocks that rattled the pane.

"Hold that thought," he said and rode his earthmoving legs around the breakfast bar and across the living room. She returned to the onion, brushing a flutter of skin from the blade. But before she could make another cut, the knife was shivered from her hand by a wail so low and close, so comprehensive, that it seemed to come from inside her, hollowing her stomach and filling her lungs as it cycled up her neck and scalp. The knife clattered to a stop. Her arms were flinched and frozen. That the wail had been human she recognized only when she looked up to see Clay's silhouette struck and kneeling in the doorway. On the steps outside, two men in full-dress military uniforms blinked grimly in the sun. The first man had his cap lodged under his arm. The second held a thin, dark box and a folded flag.

This time Clay managed to find words.

"Oh, no! Oh, Jesus!"

If he had cried her name, she would have disappeared—out a back door, if necessary, finding a way to blame him for the awkwardness, the presumption. It was that he had nobody to call to, that he was alone in the waste the world had made around him, that broke her forth and sent her running to him.

IN THIS PROCEDURE

IN THIS PROCEDURE, Ladies and Gentlemen, we will attempt to locate and remove the patient's resentment.

Resentment often manifests as a knot of gristle beneath the jaw, sometimes a lump or node against the spine, and I have marked a typical spot for incision at the seventh dorsal vertebra. Patient is forty-one years of age, male. No known allergies. A history of dyspepsia, memory loss, and rage. The pre-op log shows that a double course of anesthesia was required to stop the patient from gritting his teeth. Certainly, he's still conscious; that is both medically advised and the order of the court.

Because the condition in question is terminal if not cured, we need not be unduly wary about severing nerves and shredding connective tissue during the initial incision from dorsal seven to cervical six. I prefer a jab-and-pull technique, as such, a fairly strenuous maneuver requiring a certain amount of arm strength, which lays the spine and scapular integuments open to view. Suction, please. If caught early, as the abstract in your folders explains, resentment can be treated with an aggressive regimen of B-complex vitamins and inpatient compassion, but our subject has manifested late-stage symptoms of the disease for most of his adult life, so more invasive measures were clearly indicated. On the salmon-colored sheet, you will find summaries of several incidents that suggest the progressive state of the syndrome, including a link to surveillance video in which the patient tips over and repeatedly kicks a shopping cart with a wobbly wheel, stopping only when he has broken four toes, and you see

me now rooting around fairly liberally with a Crimean forceps for the cal-
cified root of this puling discontent.

Resentment may alternately reside in a migrated bolus or clot. In an
instance like this, where we are forced to open the leaves of the back like a
book to skim for the irregularity, advanced staunching performed by teams
of three is necessary. I'll step back to show you that we've uncovered no
visible sign of the disorder here. But do you smell it? It's the fishy, corrupt
smell underneath the iron tang of blood. So we approach, though we do
not yet enter, the realm of radical measures. In a less advanced case, where
the patient's first thought upon waking each morning was not hatred for
the middle-school baseball coach who twenty-two years ago nicknamed
him *asswipe,* it might be possible to close up and go home, recommend
chemical paralysis and assisted living, but urinalysis and the M.M.P.I. both
indicate toxic levels of rancor, multiple organs compromised by a storm of
umbrage, so we proceed with the indignectomy.

With a No. 2 Balkan augur, then, I bore a channel with some haste
directly into the mandible, through the skin and subcutaneous matter one
inch inferior to the earlobe, reducing to powder the finely knitted bones
there where the problem possibly lies. Inspecting the bore hole in vain for
a filmy lump or residue, we now repeat the procedure on the contralat-
eral side. Clean goggles, please. I now separate the inferior maxillary bone
from the skull with a Rwandan wedge and a series of controlled ham-
mer blows. A long and painful course of plastic surgery will repair some
of the damage done here if the patient survives, but cosmetic concerns
are secondary; our patient would have been dead within days had he not
been detained and sentenced to our care. The poisoning of pigeons on his
lunch hour, you'll see on the goldenrod arrest history, occasioned his last
of many involvements with the judicial system. Before that, the hate mail
to the Vice-President and the Vice-President's wife. And the rear pocket
of your folder contains the relevant sections of the patient's termination
report for sexual harassment and identity theft, committed after he suspected a coworker of eating his leftover pizza from the staff refrigerator.
Given the dire nature of these episodes, it is particularly unfortunate that
we have, as you see, once again failed to locate the source of the disease.

And so, with a Macedonian bone saw, I notch the pelvis on either
side to facilitate removal of the genitals. A standard scalpel applied cir-
cumferentially finishes the job nicely, and if I can ask you to bring me
that specimen tray, young man, we'll send the excised matter to the lab
for immediate biopsy. We'll need a specific density test on the pulverized

testicular matter, a centrifugal analysis of the remaining tissue to target deposits of gall and acrimony. It should be obvious that these tests are catastrophic and allow no possibility of reconstruction, but of what utility are his sexual organs to a person who has only masturbated for the last decade? Who admits that every woman above the age of eleven frightens him? Moreover, would it even be ethical to allow their further use to a man who once wrote *Rape my boss* on a to-do list? These are the kinds of decisions they can't teach you to make in medical school.

And so we see that the tests have come back inconclusive. Note the elevated though not abnormal levels of spite and abhorrence as we click to the next slide. The weak positive for neoplastic venom. Gentlemen, the best efforts of modern science are sometimes in vain. Therefore, I will now perform the expedient mandated in such cases by Louisiana law and termi- nate the patient with a gunshot to the heart. Cover your ears. And there. Nurse, please note the time of death. In the interests of thoroughness we'll send the brain for analysis, though experience suggests his brain will look much like yours or mine, will share the same essential shape and texture, the same concealed and foggy corners. Somewhere in him is the thing that killed him. It's best to remember that he was dying when he came to us.

ARMS

SHE WAS BLINDED by rage for the president.

That was a cliché, *blinded by rage,* but Joey knew that's how he had gotten so close to Kell: her vision was steamed over by anger, and she hadn't been able to detect his approach. He had walked right through the barbed wire and guard dogs of Kell, the foxholes and mines, and begun to do what he had been doing for a week now—sleeping with her—without her notice. What men her age didn't see was that Kell's arsenal was not there to defend her body. Her targets were long-range and her body a neglected thing, too local to hold her interest. Joey had never made love with a woman so poorly groomed, with such pronounced body odor. He'd never known a woman whose diet was so bad, whose posture was so careless she seemed to be intentionally wrecking her skeleton. The first time they'd gone to bed together (after a talk she'd dragged him to at the community college about Sunni Islam), his senses had disengaged themselves a little from the reality of Kell's body, the way they did in a public bathroom.

On this, their second weekend together, Joey had come over to her house with a vague notion of rousing her from her yellow couch and getting her out into the sunlight—he pictured her ducking snowballs with rosy cheeks—but she was locked into *Meet the Press,* rabid at distant figureheads.

"This fucker. This fucking evil fucker." Dick Cheney was asserting through his tilted grimace that the troop surge had succeeded in securing Baghdad and turning the tide of the war, which commanders on the ground were optimistic could still be won. Kell had draped herself across Joey's lap, her body open to him and her face turned away, and he was undoing the buttons of her blouse. Only women who bought their clothes at thrift stores had buttons on their blouses anymore. "Ask him about Iran, Tim. Make him respond to Sy Hersh."

She pronounced it international-style, *ee-rahn*. Joey nodded in a way that would allow Kell to feel the affirmative motion of his torso as he began to trace her nipple through her bra. This was his usual response to her politics, a rueful nodding that allowed her to believe he shared her views while at the same time allowing him to believe he hadn't really lied to her. Joey felt about President Bush and his sidekicks the way he felt about all people who forced themselves into the public eye: they were brazen liars, but what did you expect? People who were honest about themselves and the world didn't make speeches. So maybe there was a sense in which Joey had misrepresented himself into Kell's affections. But there was another sense—evidenced by the way she unfastened her bra for him even as she yelled at the TV—in which Kell understood and accepted the terms of their relationship.

"He makes me hope there's a hell," she said with her very secular mouth. Kell's lips were thin and colorless, without the least hint of luxury, and in this way they fit her face, which had gathered a sparse dust of soil over an ancestry of rocky famine. Forbidding as it was, Kell's face attracted Joey the way all freckled things did, seeming marred for his special regard. Her field-brown hair completed the untended landscape of her face, its weeds bound up in a windy ponytail. She had almost no breasts, which he hadn't expected to like but did, and the belly and hip his hand now tracked in its descent had the spare immediacy of a body which, although it had performed the offices of a woman's, was essentially still a girl's.

"Why is Tim being so goddamn deferential?" she asked as Joey slipped a finger inside her. Joey didn't know. On their way to bed, they stopped at the crib to look at Marina. Eight months old, she lay in the beatific daze that seemed to be the hallmark of that age, her limbs performing soft spasms in response to the twisting mobile above her. When he looked at the baby, Joey felt half asleep too, not unpleasantly so. Everything outside the house went fuzzy and unimportant. He thought of his parents and friends with forgiveness. In the slow self-education of Marina's blinking, he read a message about the forward crawl of human history.

When Kell undressed this time, her naked smell caught him by surprise—it was as sharp as always, but it was a sharpness he knew now, like a foreign spice his brain had made a place for.

JOEY LIKED science fiction. Not the time-travel and alien-worlds stuff, but novels about machine dystopia or world revolution through the Internet. He had just finished a book about drug apocalypse that was causing him to notice all the prescription medications people took. He was fifty pages into a new one about a white supremacist who disrupted black people's brain functions with cell phone signals. *Kell* was short for something, he assumed, but he hadn't asked because he liked its speculative feel, the way it suggested a personality loosed from the bonds of the present.

He had never dated an angry woman before. He had dated frightened women. He had dated sweet women whose kindness he couldn't live up to. For six months he had gone out with a heavy woman who kept her embarrassment held so tight against her that there was no room for him. But Kell was never embarrassed. She outsourced her embarrassment to the people around her, often Joey, who felt himself redden when she screamed *muthafucka!* in traffic or kicked over her kitchen garbage can because it had stubbed her toe. She had an undiluted anger on the topic of her marriage, a mistake undertaken at eighteen and abandoned at twenty-two that Joey had heard her blame variously on patriarchy, economic conditions, Hollywood, and her *fucking hormones.* She hated any company big enough to be called a corporation. The government was full of rich thieves and ultimately the source of all problems. The physical world was constantly defying her. The way she said *I'm off to the chain gang* when she left for work suggested that she saw her job at the grocery store as a punishment imposed by some larger force. Only Marina escaped Kell's ire, sealed in a cooing biosphere exempt from the raging storms without. So few people knew how they really felt, and in this sense Kell's anger was magnetic; it drew the loose filings of the world and aimed them in one direction. Joey was a cook at the hospital, and after Kell flung a pot of scorched rice into the back yard, its brown grains dotting the snow like cinnamon, he took over the job of making dinner.

Plus, there was always the chance he might say or do the thing that would unlock the strongbox of her heart and convince her to spend its contents on him.

He liked the way she looked in her work uniform, all that too-tight polyester brown, and he had some vague idea of showing support, so he went to the store during her shift.

"Fuck are you doing?" she whispered, her eyes furtive, as if he had just shoplifted. He looked at his hands to make sure he hadn't.

"Getting stuff for mashed potatoes."

"Nnnnh, Joey," knitting her brow as if he had caused her a sudden unsupportable migraine. She aimed the top of her head at him and started tugging his things across the scanner.

The other four registers were run by black girls with elaborately curled hair and nails. Even in their crappy Midwest town, there was a minority underclass of garbage men, road workers, and check-out girls. The customer behind Joey butted the orange divider up against his pint of whole milk. Somewhere a cart wheel rattled. Joey was distracted from appraising the curve of Kell's ass in her work pants by her exasperated flipping of the laminated cards with the codes for produce. The surprise of his visit had made her forget the code for potatoes, that most everyday of vegetables, and by the time she got his items totaled and bagged, his idea to come here seemed as dumb and flimsy as the single plastic sack in his cart.

"Is it always this busy?"

"Four dollars and twelve cents."

"I guess I'll see you later."

"Have a nice day, Sir." She gave him the top of her head again as she began the next order, her scalp bisected by a combed part of perfect, pale exactness.

THEY WENT TO a club with some of her friends. Tim wore Goth makeup and had a beer belly. Vicki was a wan, wordless girl who seemed deficient in protein and never looked up from the table. Buzzy was gay, a fact he foregrounded by lilting his hand against Joey's upper arm and feyly cooing, *Ooh, he's tall!* Joey recognized Buzzy's thorny orange flattop and the jagged darkness of the club for the imitation menaces they were. Imitations of menace were the best their town could manage, a thought whose completed shape felt like something securely tucked in the pocket of his mind. Somehow he knew, from a slumped sameness in their bodies, that Kell and her friends had been coming here since they were the age of the fake-ID kids crashing together on the dance floor. This is where they had huddled while time besieged them, and they looked a little disappointed by the discovery that they had somehow survived and were now twenty-three.

Joey was so out of place here—he was thirty-one and wearing a baseball cap with a trout on it—that he found himself enjoying the inner calm of the total misfit.

"Everybody, this is Joey."

They greeted him casually, but the ensuing silence suggested that Kell's bringing a man into public was not a casual occurrence.

"We met at the costume shop," Joey ventured.

Kell leaned over the table and yelled through the music.

"I was six bucks short on this honeybee costume for Marina? Joey just gave it to me out of the blue. They wanted twenty-five bucks for that fucking costume."

A week ago Saturday had been Halloween. The hospital kitchen staff had voted to dress to a seventies theme, and Joey had been shopping for an Afro.

"You cook at the hospital? That's cool," they agreed, and something in the slack solidarity of their nodding suggested that they liked him better for not having a job of real position and expertise—head chef in a restaurant, for example, the job Joey eventually hoped to have.

"I condemn racial stereotypes," Tim yelled. It was such a dorky thing to say, and Tim obviously felt so stupid for saying it even though he had spent two minutes working up the phrasing, that Joey's feelings toward him turned tender.

"It was an equal-opportunity Afro," Joey specified. "Strawberry blonde."

Vicki grinned at the table.

"How did you get your hair net on?" Buzzy quipped, which Joey thought was genuinely funny. "I went as Princess Diana," Buzzy continued before Joey could answer. "In my *mind*."

"This town doesn't know how to do Halloween," Tim deprecated with his ghoul's mouth.

"Wait," Kell said, "so the way to 'do Halloween' is staying home and renting *Ten Things I Hate about You*?"

"I told you, I'm not going to be the only person dressing up."

"There were parties. There was a party right fucking here."

"Did I know about them?"

"Did you show any initiative and find out about them? Did you behave like someone who had an actual interest in socially participating?"

"You're being unrealistic."

Joey could see that Tim was a person who, if badgered, would be unable to stop his voice from leaping up into his sinuses with a bullied wail. Buzzy came to his rescue.

"I agree with Timmy. A hunnert percent. This town does suck. It sucks long and hard and sloppy. It sucks inadequately, without providing orgasm. I saw New York and New Orleans on the news? Their Halloween? *Hel*-lo."

"Joey, what do you think?" Vicki asked, raising her eyes for the briefest moment, an act that required the sum total of her courage and brushed a soft feather against Joey's heart. He liked Halloween, he said, but he had noticed that people who championed Halloween were usually people who held special grudges against the other holidays, people who had taught themselves to champion it by conscious process. As for New York and New Orleans, he said, those places were exaggerated by definition. "It's what they're about. The wow."

"*New York and New Orleans, New York and New Orleans,*" Kell parroted. "That's your answer for everything, Buzzy. Why don't you just fucking go there?"

"See, Joey, I haven't given up, so I'm an object of ridicule."

"Given up on what?"

"I sing and act."

Once every year or two, Joey met a person he knew would be important to his life, and he could tell when this was happening because the person snapped into a prepared spot in his mind like a puzzle piece in a larger picture he could now smooth his hand over. Buzzy was one of those people. As Buzzy described the demo CD he was mailing to agents, he took on full detail for Joey: his acne-scarred forehead, his stubby old-man's nose, the childish smallness of his hands, the anxiety of his leg under the table, which sent residual shimmies through his shoulders. *Sing* probably meant singing the *Mulan* theme to a karaoke machine, and *act* probably meant reciting Scarlett O'Hara lines in front of the mirror, but these things seemed fitting to the total person of Buzzy, somehow not dreary and desperate like Tim's mascara. Buzzy's dreams might be pink and coated with candy, but he would know how to spit them out before they ruined his teeth. On a hunch Joey asked him, "What was Kell like as a kid?"

"Lipstick and TEA PARTIES!" Buzzy gushed, finding something delicious in the question. "She made me play house, and she would send my ass out to work with a briefcase. And when I got home, quote-quote, she had one of those talking dolls? She would make it cry when I touched it so she could take it from me and, like, comfort it."

Kell shrugged sheepishly at this report of her girlish sadism. "You were a terrible father, dude."

"All that early emasculation. We can see how *that* turned out."

"What do you do?" Joey asked.

"I work in a DAYCARE," Buzzy said, displaying his middle fingers to Kell.

Everyone except Joey got up to dance, even Vicki, her arms hanging forgotten at her sides as her feet padded carefully in tennis shoes, and the music rose in volume until it disappeared, and Joey must have fallen asleep because Kell was pulling his earlobe and everyone was breathing heavily and aiming straws at their mouths.

On the way home, as Kell wrestled the big wheel of her outdated Buick, Joey wondered why he had never found a woman's arms attractive before. Kell's were lithe and beautifully muscled, shining in the dark.

"You have really nice arms."

"Dude, are you leching on my *arms?*"

"They're pretty."

"You want to fuck when we get home?"

"Sure, OK." The car mumbled thoughtfully beneath them. "Kell, why do you say *fuck* so much?"

Her head cannied back a degree: "What the hell, are you criticizing my vocabulary, yo?" She sometimes used hip-hop lingo for emphasis. She did this without irony, so that's how Joey took it.

"Not criticizing."

"What, do you find it *indelicate?*"

The sneer folded inside the little-girl voice she used made it impossible for Joey to say yes, which might not have been his answer anyway. She was making it into a question of gender, which it wasn't. It was a question of contamination. The word *fuck* was like a car alarm that wouldn't stop going off in the street or a horror film with multiple spillings of blood—it threw a kind of dirt across the clean walls Joey hoped to build around his life.

"I don't know who you think I am, Joey," Kell said, thunking the car into PARK in her mother's driveway. She had apparently played out several more steps of the conversation in her mind and gotten herself upset. Joey had to stand up out of the car to hear what she said next because she had jumped out, slammed her door, and aimed her perpetual motion toward the porch, talking as she went. "I mean, that's lame-ass shit, Joey. 'Why do you say *fuck* so much.'"

"But answer the question," he said, his chin resting on the car's metal roof. She turned, sighing with extreme exhaustion, as if his sedulous idiocy had just put all the cells of her body to sleep. "You with your pretty arms, there."

The frustration on Kell's face suggested that Joey had violated the rules of conversation so unacceptably that, if she only had the means, she would hack off her own arms to prove it.

"You're so fucking retarded, Joey. Wait in the car while I get Marina."

Maybe he was. Retarded, in some sense. One of them must be. But that only meant whoever it was needed the other one's help and protection.

PHYSICAL THINGS were a source of frustration for Kell, but Joey was good at physical things, he was a person who accomplished things with his hands, so he checked the air pressure in her tires and vacuumed her floor mats, he re-glued a curl of linoleum in the kitchen. Although Kell's words were always set to attack mode, she hated actual confrontation, so it was Joey who asked the neighbor to give back the garbage can he had taken. Joey could not get Kell to sit down at the table for a proper meal—the formality of plates and silverware, she said, smothered her—but when he made stuffed mushrooms and left the tray on the stove, she ate all of them standing there with a hand cupped under her chin. Her sex was the same way—full of frowning concentration and a sense of forcing things into place. Even the way she held Marina looked secondhand, learned from a book, the way some people always had to use a recipe when they cooked. And when Marina got sick, three days of diarrhea and listless crying, Kell was as jumpy and withdrawn as a lab animal subjected to random shocks.

Glancing into the car beside him at a stoplight, Joey saw Buzzy's red mace of a head.

Hey, Joey mouthed, raising his hand.

Hi!, Buzzy mouthed back, and they kind of smiled and nodded patiently until the green light pulled them out of sync. The mood inside Joey's car had been lightened by the chance encounter, and he drifted along contentedly, past auto parts stores and check-cashing huts, until the next light slowed him and he glanced left to see Buzzy once again beside him. They laughed and shrugged behind closed glass, raising wry hands at the situation around them as if to suggest that sitting at a red light when there were no other cars in view was a silly modern moment they were above. When the light changed, they hunched over their steering wheels and pretended to drag race at twenty miles per hour. It was no surprise to Joey when they turned into the same parking lot.

"Something with pictures for me, please," Buzzy tweeted as he held open the door of the bookstore they had both come to.

They paused inside to allow themselves a moment of commercial lordship, breathing in the sweet-sour tang of publishing, then Joey followed Buzzy to EDUCATION AND STUDY GUIDES, where Buzzy knelt before a shelf of math workbooks, his scalp pallidly gleaming through the stalagmites of his hair. When Buzzy stood, Joey saw that he had slipped on a pair of reading glasses; though vintage and purple, they nevertheless tamed Buzzy's face into an echo of all toilers and squinters through history.

Buzzy play-acted a scene of whisking a book behind his back, as if Joey had taken him by surprise; and then, as if he had been broken by tough interrogation, he relented and showed Joey the object of his shame.

"I'm getting my Gen Ed courses out of the way at Neosha," Buzzy said, naming the community college in town. "They have me in Algebra II."

"What are you going to study? For a major?"

Buzzy described his plan to earn a degree in counseling and psychology at a university in the city two hours away, and he did so with a lack of fuss and gesture that convinced Joey that he would, in fact, do it.

"Well, you need the algebra because if you're counseling three people and then you start to counsel two more, how many does that make?"

"Excellent point."

Joey gave up his fake paging of a gardening book.

"Tell me about the ex-husband."

"Poor bastard didn't stand a chance."

This answer was so different from what Joey had expected that he could only wait in silence for Buzzy to continue.

"I don't even think he pays child support anymore. I mean, he tried, but she wouldn't cash the checks. Paul," Buzzy said, realizing he had neglected to put first things first. "Paul, and he was valedictorian of our class. She was number two, by the way. I doubt she told you that. They were Editor and Assistant Editor of the newspaper. Student Council President and Student Body President. They were one of those high school couples where you look at them and feel hopeful about the world."

Joey could easily picture all of this because everyone in their town went to the same high school: Kell brainstorming headlines in the newspaper office with Mr. Shaeffer and his walrus mustache; Kell shaking Principal McMichael's hand and returning to her auditorium seat with the salutatorian's crystal trophy. Joey knew the exact smells and colors of the place where those things had happened, the textures of the tile and carpet.

"Paul had scholarships—they both did—but when she got pregnant, he stayed here to work. This was a pudgy little boy, Joey, littler than me, and he got a job at Dressler." Dressler was a tool box factory on the edge of town, a byword for union breaking and greasy exertion. "Getting married was the mistake part." Buzzy concentrated on the next sentence, his eyes looking at nothing until he had the words he wanted. "It was like she had him on a rope, and she kept pulling him in and hitting him." He performed the gesture, tugging and punching, tugging and punching.

"She blamed him for the pregnancy?"

"Well, sort of," squinting one eye behind its lens, as if this characterization would work as well as any for a truth that was a lot less simple.

Joey raised his eyes suddenly from Buzzy's book.

"This isn't that child." The math of it hit him. "The one she got pregnant with."

Buzzy closed his eyes and nodded subtly, as if Joey was closing in on the essential secret.

"She gave the first one up for adoption. Marina's their second. She got pregnant and filed for divorce."

The noisy hush of books rose up around them. Joey was about to redirect his steps to PARENTING AND CHILDCARE when two thoughts came together in his head.

"Buzzy, you probably know. What's a kid supposed to be eating at eight months?"

Buzzy was slowly but firmly shaking his head before Joey could even finish his sentence.

"No way. Leave me out of this." Buzzy patted the cover of the algebra book to indicate that his shopping was done, then tipped his head at the bathroom door. "Got to check my messages."

It was one of the stranger euphemisms Joey had heard for taking a pee. Not until after midnight, lying awake with Kell's furious liquids evaporating from his skin, did Joey realize that Buzzy had been speaking literally, that for some people in their town, finding love meant leaving messages in a toilet stall and sneaking back hopefully for a reply.

KELL EVEN hated the way the president walked to a podium.

"He actually thinks he's a cowboy." Joey, glancing over his shoulder from the stove, saw nothing more than a man who looked uncomfortable in a suit. Anyway, Kell's kitchen TV was too small, half the size of the toaster it sat next to, to convey the motives of the people on its screen. "Like some code of Western manliness is going to make this Blackwater shit acceptable." Joey pulled out the oven rack, eyeballs in the heat, and slid a knife into the chicken. "And what movie did he learn that fucking squint from?"

Kell knew inside information about every topic the president discussed, and she kept interjecting this information as Joey checked the rice, added balsamic vinegar to the dressing he was making, then capped the dressing and shook it to a uniform oily umber. Kell subscribed to serious magazines and always had three or four of them folded open in the living room, which is how she knew to say things like *One hundred eighty thousand private contractors operating outside the rules of the military, and you couldn't see this coming?* But why did she want to know things that gave her no pleasure? Everything she learned made her more unhappy. It wasn't like forcing herself to drink bad-tasting medicine because it didn't make her well. It wasn't like eating bland but healthy food because it didn't make her stronger. Her life was more crushed by faraway ideas every day. Some other version of her, an imaginary Kell with notes clutched to her chest, was peppering the president with tough questions at a news conference, but the version she actually inhabited wouldn't allow itself the comfort of plates and silverware.

Joey set a bowl of salad in front of her. Her eyes stayed on the TV, and her hands continued their work on Marina's high-chair tray, where she was shaving slivers off a candy bar with a dull knife. The chicken in its gurgle of sauce was ready and would wait in the oven until they finished their salads, but Joey reached in with a spoon and nipped off the end of one breast, put it on a dessert plate, and scooped a spoonful of the sauce over it. Crushing the meat into reddish scraps with a spoon and blowing over the dish to cool it, he turned and set the plate in front of Marina, gathering up the shards of candy with his other hand and carrying them to the garbage.

"The fuck are you doing?"

"She needs real food."

Marina was going to cry, Joey saw, as soon as her struggling brain could assemble the cause.

"Who says?"

"Buzzy. And some books I looked at."

Kell nocked a breath and drew it back to full tension, pausing to decide whether Joey was worth it or not, then sent it flying home to his breast.

"You fucking fuck. Is she your fucking kid, yo? She's not your fucking kid." Each sentence set its torch to the next, the mob of Kell's ire gathering force. "You warped motherfucker. Who the fuck do you think you are?"

In truth, he did not know. He was a person with praiseworthy goals who had acquired a certain wisdom in life, or he was a pathetic, lonely man who had wasted his chances. He was someone who reflected the basic humanity of everyone he met, or he was a person who sentimentalized all his relationships into dimwit fiction. Cruelly, his body chose this moment to replay its memories of Kell, the lean circumference of her rib cage in his hands, the gristle of her lower lip against his—his senses commemorating what his brain had just made impossible to have—and he jumped up from his chair as much to shake free of these images as to snatch his keys from the counter.

On this cue Marina loosed her grief, and Kell released her own flood at Joey's back as he grabbed his jacket from the living room, where a larger version of the president was apparently telling lie after lie.

"You have no idea how to behave. It's so deeply fucked."

The screen door was on a tight spring, and knowing she'd want to follow him outside to continue her points, he waited and passed the door into her hand.

"You've got all these bourgeois ideas you can't articulate. Why don't you mow my fucking lawn, bitch. Why don't, hey, let's go jogging, in jogging suits. Then we'll go to Disney."

He stepped down into the driveway. He'd always hated the intimate, gnashing sound of gravel, the way it spat and snickered underfoot at the human folly taking place above it.

"Look, everybody, it's Mr. Joey." Without responses to lock onto, her sentences were fizzing out of control, looping on themselves. "Wow, he's so wise. He's, let's sit at his feet and learn what to eat and how to act."

He had to open the car door in stages because Kell was standing in the way, their feet shuffling and reshuffling until the machine finally contained him. She pounded the window until he rolled it down and then kept going, chewing the air between them as he fluttered his key ring for the correct key.

"Don't you *ever* fucking touch my baby's food, or my baby." He could somehow feel the crush of her grip on the doorsill. "You hear me, motherfucker?"

Then, as he fitted the key into the ignition, she spilled over from his peripheral vision and filled the car, breaking off the turn-signal stem as she fought her way across the steering wheel. The lights from the house suffused the edges of her body, its slim silhouette held in midair by the double buttress of her arms sweeping out to lock his right wrist in a stony grip.

"Joey! God damn it!"

Here he was looking at the top of her head again. He let go of the ignition and turned her over so he could see her face, struggling her the rest of the way into the car until her rear end plopped into his lap. The flush of exertion had drowned her freckles. Her chest heaved desperately, but it was not the kind of desperation that yields to laughing or crying. She was angry at something it could take him years to find.

How to Be a Better You

YOUR LIFE IS REPLETE with inefficiencies. As your Eubios consultants, it is our obligation to state this plainly so you can face the problem clearly. Remember the DVD we played at your Orientation: Only by appraising yourself with a critical eye can you hope to achieve a life of meaning and focus instead of the life of shame and doubt your self-survey indicates. To this end, the Expanded Mid-Term Report you hold in your hands— a special amenity reserved for our Total Being members—moves beyond the physical to address the interpersonal, personal, and inner-personal. Of twelve possible Spheres of Waste, it has been determined that you inhabit twelve. Total remediation could possibly be the work of years. But when your aunt enrolled you as a Eubios member, she stated her belief that inside you was a better you she knew you could be, a you you could be proud of. You have stated that you agree. You will take the first step toward that you when you open this Report and begin reading. Please notice the Reflection Questions on the attached page.

Of all your compromised Life Areas, the one most characteristic of your particular manner of wasting is Self-Cleaning, specifically Showering. Consider: If you are inefficient in your most private moments, when you are in your own best care, how can you hope to practice efficiency in the larger world? The following data, compiled from twenty-two visits to the lavatory space by your Eubios Field Squad, reveal, first, that you commonly stray from your task before you begin it by activating a small television beside the unused second sink of your vanity. If you submit a

Pledge Card committing to choose a single channel and leave the television tuned to it while you shave, we will not mandate its removal in our Final Report. However, our observations show that you change the channel, on average, 37 times per morning, a practice that requires not only the time to manually retrieve the remote—2 to 3 seconds, during which time shaving is suspended—but also the time to dry your hand before you retrieve the remote, or to dry the remote after you use it, followed by a moment of neural paralysis as your visual field reorients itself to the new arrangement of scrolling scores and text boxes that characterize the news and sports programs you prefer, a hiatus during which you not only cannot further the act of shaving but also cannot successfully absorb information. A current-events post-test showed that you "get" almost none of what you see: Questions you missed included "Who is Vice-President of the United States?," "Who is in first place in any division of baseball?," and "Who or what is Fallujah?" As importantly, human cognition studies show not only that "surfing" produces information handicap but also that it yields no net gain of pleasure. And you have reported that you hate all your favorite TV channels. At a cost of three minutes per day—0.003% of your daily consciousness plenum and 460 hours over the balance of your life—you will agree that the price of your bathroom viewing habits is too high.

The focus you show undressing and entering the shower is excellent. Initial wetting, beyond reproach. But our Video Lifebrary shows that you consistently utilize up-and-down soaping. Our policy is circular soaping. This is just scientific. A more serious problem is your practice of saving and combining the shards of soap that remain when each bar melts or breaks. Nine times in June you bent and groped for soap fragments when they split from the larger bar you had melded them to. The economic benefit of this practice is nearly unmeasurable in whole numbers, and the reminder of human frailty occasioned by squatting naked in a wet receptacle constitutes an unacceptable debit from your self-esteem. As for crossing your arms, closing your eyes, and just making bubbling noises for several minutes as the water streams over your face, we will be equipping you with skills designed to make the rest of your day an experience you will not be compelled to postpone with this and other forms of flagrant stalling.

Other irregularities will require lengthy review (for example, the use of three different brushes for your hair), but most fall within the plus-or-minus two percentage points we allow for Idiosyncrasy. In summary of your effectiveness at Morning Toilet, our conclusion is that missteps force you to rush and blunder the central act, with the result that you often fail to wash portions of your body (left armpit 14 times, anterior genitals 5 times), and that you are not a very clean person.

Installation of a Classis II-Series HauteCoacher ($1999) will eliminate those time-wasting moments of standing in front of your closet and hating every piece of clothing you own.

At Eubios we like to say that what you hope to avoid is the feeling of traveling in circles, a condition we call *déjà you*. Of finding yourself back at point A one year older, two years older. Of asking, Why haven't I grown? What happened to my resolutions? Your aunt listed as her most significant concern for you your frequent change of profession. Our work with excellence metrics and Feck Theory suggests that the American average of five career changes is detrimental to self and society, so you must see that, with six jobs in the last ten months, you are doing pronounced harm to yourself. We have enclosed and ask you to consider a brochure detailing our CPR (Career Path Resuscitation) Program, a patented system of marionette strings, ventriloquism, and light electrical discouragements that has provided many of our clients with relief.

In the meantime, please note the following recommendations regarding two areas of your Work Life. First, we urge you in the strongest possible terms to begin telling the truth. Like public speaking or singing on key, truthfulness is a talent not everyone has; being among the have-nots, you will need to think of truth as a skill you can develop, like typing or archery, a competency you can acquire through drill and practice. From the indirect dishonesty of playing Chuzzle for an entire eight-hour work shift to the direct, unusual lies you tell co-workers—that you have a Siamese twin, for example—a large part of your day is spent in mild to gross falsehood. You do not own a racing motorcycle capable of speeds exceeding 175 miles per hour. The discoloration on your cheek is a birthmark, not a scar from frostbite suffered on the south face of K10. You were not a child-master of Hatha yoga. Eubios consultants in the client workplace obey a strict policy of observant non-participation; but our commitment to that policy has never been more seriously tested than on the day you told your supervisor you had leukemia. We yearned to take you aside and produce from our accordion folder the Satisfaction and Outcome tables on lying, which show lying to be one of the least fulfilling of human activities. We wanted to brief you on recent scholarship in the epidemiology of lying, which finds that the statistical spread and damage of a lie makes telling one much like coughing a communicable disease into the faces of those around you. Moreover, instruments under development in our lab reveal as yet unexplained gray deposits left by lies upon the soul. But we maintained our stance of observant non-participation as you employed the terminology you had gathered that morning from WebMD to perpetrate your lie and as Jennie M., your supervisor, reached across the desk in tears to take your hand. As you embellished and consolidated your story through the day for the consumption of your colleagues, we watched and waited. Even an individual like yourself with Social Intelligence scores in the 20th percentile must see that this lie (not told toward any purpose our observations could uncover) will follow you for the remainder of your tenure at this job and cost you many hours of maintenance. What you do not see, but must be convinced of, is that inefficiency is unhappiness. And that there is something other than unhappiness to be lived. We assure you there is! Happiness is real! We can show you the graphs.

Meanwhile, here is a second, more easily addressed Work Flaw you can remediate before we get our equipment set up: you have very, very poor mouse skills. You frequently Minimize when you mean to Restore and Restore when you mean to X-out. Also, please realize that since your fingers are already on the keyboard when you type a search topic, hitting "Enter" is a more expeditious way to begin that search than lifting your right hand from the keyboard, securing the mouse, wiggling it to locate the cursor, and zeroing in on the tiny "Go" button. Finally, most unnecessarily, you double-click online. This superfluity arises from failing to recognize the difference between word processing and navigating the Internet. To prevent accidentally disappearing screens and unintended double purchases, as well as to quiet office rumors that you lack the basic skills for your job, please take our word that a single click will activate any online link. Also, find a quiet moment to remedy your fear or ignorance of the right-click, which contains many useful functions to speed your workplace tasks.

Think of it this way: every object in the world contains not only utility but also waste. The waste of considering it, cleaning it, repairing it, of insuring and storing it. If you imagine a complex of lines emanating from every object to represent the ways it relates to other objects and intersects with the life of man—in short, all its physical and metaphysical possibilities—you will have some idea of the web of associations waiting to trap and dissolve the modern mind. The Mentis 2.1 Diagnostic Brainchip that our technicians installed in your medulla reveals a mind so distracted by thought options that it can no longer choose. We see this frequently. There is a sense that all thoughts can now be thought and that thinking them doesn't hurt enough to make not thinking them necessary. And a further sense that the traditional duties of the mind—weighing, discerning, deciding—are too arduous and, like cooking and walking, best left to people of the past. How can you know, for example, how seriously to take your aunt's cancer? In an age when they can just remove her ovaries? In a day when, if you just sit in front of the TV long enough, Mandy Patinkin will offer the precise -trex, -brex, or -statin for her problem? In a time when she mostly won't feel any of what they do to her anyway?

As an opening thread, these thoughts, taken from your Brainscript of last Monday, are acceptably coherent. But taking the five minutes of cognitive activity that succeed these ruminations concerning your aunt, we find significant cause for worry: Twenty seconds wondering whether your middle finger, when you raise it in traffic, makes its point with proper force since it is shorter than your index finger and not of impressive thickness. Did people seeing your middle finger infer inadequacy in you as a person and a man? Could they even see you and your finger behind your tinted windows? Ten seconds flexing the finger and wondering whether a finger could be strengthened and enhanced like a biceps, then forty-five seconds imagining the accidents that might befall or be caused by a man with superhumanly strong fingers—tearing open his own nose while picking it, driving ink pens straight through the credit card slips he was signing and into the laminated sales counters beneath, pulverizing the clitorises of the women who would beg him to fingerbang them when word about his extreme digits got out—and then typing a few words really hard just to get the feel of what that would be like. A minute and fifteen seconds plotting when you would next masturbate. Ten seconds: *Did* she feel pain? If so, and she probably did because she was a very stoic lady, was it more of a stab or an ache? Or just a discomfort, not empirically worse than an upset stomach, the way the pain you felt at the dentist was bad mostly in terms of the idea of it when in reality it hurt more to pull a hangnail? Eight seconds swearing to God that you could just put your head down on the keyboard and fall asleep, nonsense trailing across the screen as your cheek depressed the keys. Where did other people get all their fucking energy? And how unfair was a world where it looked increasingly like you were never going to own a BMW? It's not like you were asking for a fucking Lamborghini, just a conservative Cashmere-Silver 1-Series like the one on the manufacturer's homepage, not even necessarily with the leather interior, and this willingness to compromise ought to count for something. It was a fact, common sense said so, that there were ample resources in the world for everyone to own the car of his liking—or there would be if we didn't keep dumping money into the useless black hole of Africa and Congress could get off its corrupt ass and we could finally kill off the unions. Of course there would have to be a vetting process for people receiving the vehicles, to ascertain that they weren't documentedly evil or reckless crackheads or deeply annoying to the majority sensibility in their dress, speech, and personal habits, like Jennie M. So Jennie M. enters the hearing room to make her case before the Auto Board, and guess who's behind the table. You! That's right, bitch, how do you like me now? Imagine how quickly her fat-lady bossiness would disappear when you went off-script and asked a few specially designed questions: If you were able to smell your own coffee breath, how long would it take before you threw up? True or False: The point of eating a Weight Watchers meal for lunch is lost if you eat two. What hole in your education or deep personal stupidity has allowed you to reach adulthood pronouncing the *–th* at the end of words as an *–f*, and do you know that this makes you an object of ridicule among your employees, even the ones you think are your friends, and that they often imitate you to liven up the soulless office you run? *I just saw the boss wif the regional manager. Walking Souf? Norf. I hope she brushed her teef. As long as she took a baf.* And while you had her there, you would further point out that whatever institution gave her her MBA ought to be bombed into nothingness as a sponsor of intellectual terrorism, and that last year's suits would be best left in last year's closet, in memory of the thinner woman they had once fit. Turning then to your peers on the Auto Board, you would propose that in this case no car at all should be assigned, but instead the only conveyance appropriate to the personal worth and gravity of the applicant: a clown's tricycle. Thirty seconds on how, in truth, you'd always preferred bigger women, women Jennie M.'s exact size, in fact; and that if there were some psychosurgical process by which everything that made her her could be comprehensively scoured from her interior and replaced by a personality capable of intelligent thought, she would be about the best-looking woman you could imagine, especially her calves and ankles, so sweet and fat, and you were definitely going to jerk off as soon as you got home, or maybe even right now in the company bathroom because nobody else was getting a hell of a lot done today, so what the fuck did it matter? Twenty seconds weighing the linguistic, social, and moral differences between *gray* and *grey* and reconfirming what you'd known since childhood in a way that preceded decision, that you were a steadfast *a*-person, and wondering what sort of fey sleazoid could possibly favor *e*. Sixty seconds, a long time by your standards, smarting over the injustice of a God that could create creatures capable of pain and then give them consciousness.

At Eubios it is not our business to render ethical judgments. Our business is distribution, direction, and duration. By any of these measures, the preceding Brainscript reveals a mind unable to focus on its task, i.e., preparing a spreadsheet of the average weight-per-unit of the chickens provided to the nugget-making company you work for. Your mind has the same relation to itself as a morbidly obese person who will not stop eating the potato chips he knows are killing him. Two things are true of this person. One, he will never achieve any form of success he can be content with because he must punish himself for his own self-wrecking by producing ongoing moments of failure. Two, the taste of healthy food has grown repellent to him. Like this person, your mind lives on junk-jokes and junk-ideas, junk-hopes and junk-declarations, gorging itself on the very things that make it sick. You have lost your taste for the genuine interactions that studies show sustain life and give organisms, even laboratory mice, a sense of purpose. You failed to visit your aunt, the person who raised you, each of the last three times she was in the hospital; our observations have turned up no evidence to contradict the notion that you live in stark friendlessness; and by self-reporting, you haven't performed an embrace with another human being in 210 days. At elevated levels, self-love and self-hate converge and meet at a point, graphs show. We need cite no further evidence than the 14 straight hours of "Flavor of Love" you watched on 6/9–6/10 to know that you are very near that point.

But your situation is not hopeless. We have re-skilled clients whose cases were more advanced than yours and helped them to achieve as much as three to five years of efficient and meaningful life. We specialize in small changes with large results. At the Recommendations Consult, we won't be using words like *love* and *happiness,* we'll be using words like *maid service* and *Post-it notes, alarm clock* and *direct deposit.* We believe a daily planner will help. We'll show you how to get started and stay committed. Essentially what's necessary is attaining a personal force and gravity beyond the reach of all the things you see and hear. It is often said we are in an age of efficiency. The opposite is true! A person in sympathy with the age, responding to its cues and opportunities, would explode into a million floating pieces. It is a problem of the soul now measurable by science, and only science can fix it.

Your aunt will soon be gone, William. Then all you'll have is you. Be the best you you can be!

PROFESSION OF THE BODY

I AM WATCHING a fat kid eat.

A girl this time. With none of the daintiness heavy girls sometimes affect at meals, she stokes fry after fry into the scuttle of her mouth, building steam against the last three periods of the day. Her forearms glisten. Her eyes wear a private glaze. When she giggles through her nose at something a friend has said, I root for bubbles to form—it seems almost likely in the humid cafeteria—but she claps a hand to her face, and I stand unsatisfied near the water fountain.

Her name is Haley Gill, and she is a freshman in my fourth-period class. Because she has distinguished herself in no way during the first month of school, neither by identifying parts of speech with unusual skill nor by wearing the premature makeup of a troubled home life nor by behaving badly and forcing me to speak to her in tones of quiet intimidation, I am able to think of her only in terms of her size. She plods each day to her second-row desk on calves as staunch as mortar shells and props on the under-rack of the desk in front of her loafers already jellying off their soles. Wheezing patiently from the walk to class, her budding breasts tossing like buoys in the ocean of her school uniform, she unzips her pencil case with the dimpled fingers of a Roman emperor. I let students work in pairs to liven up grammar lessons, but the only time Hayley has ever left her desk voluntarily was when she asked to go to the office and take her medicine, and the struggle she waged to get out the door gave me the sudden impression of a person sealed inside a gag-suit version of herself. This fourteen year-old, this ninth grader, is doomed.

Or is she? Alan Bauer, sitting across from her and fortifying his own soft middle with a double portion of the same fries, isn't in a position to tease her. Neither is Rod Hoffheiser, that immensity, draining his second Coke. The girl to Haley's left, Samantha-something, a sophomore, has a freakishly barreled torso that makes Haley look shapely by contrast, yet she leads, according to rumor, a successfully active sexual life with the boys of our school. The fat-kid ostracism and torture of yesteryear are over. Hayley's table, a fair sample of all the tables in the cafeteria, is a utopia for the obese, a fat kid's heaven with the gates thrown open. I stand near the whining fountain and fulfill my daily lunch duty at Our Lady of Perpetual Succor, a high school in a suburb of New Orleans, and a stew of boredom, disgust, and glee is simmering and glooping inside me by the time Missy Heaton, a P.E. teacher I would very much like to see naked, arrives to take over my post.

"Rod Hoffheiser has the body of a forty-eight year-old man," I say by way of greeting, leaning against pale blue cinderblocks in the general noise. "He's got bigger tits than you."

"You're bad!" she says appreciatively.

"I mean, really. What the heck are y'all doing in gym class?"

"It's the health unit right now." She nudges me to signal in advance that she is joking: "Are you saying my students don't look healthy?"

Missy is easy to flirt with because she is twenty-eight and not married, which qualifies as a disaster to her and means she is constantly attuned to making herself pleasing to men. At forty-five, however—and as a complete alien to Missy politically, socially, and physically—I am not a realistic option, and this combination of factors makes us safe for, and irresistible to, each other. Along with her usual platonic friskiness, Missy's words contain an allusion to my position as our liaison for the Healthy Children Act, a law requiring schools to collect physical data on their student populations and to scrutinize the school's health, physical education, and lunch programs with a goal of lowering the national index of youth obesity, which, as I well know, is at 15% and rising. As a private school, Perpetual Succor could have opted out, but opting in brought us twelve thousand federal dollars a year.

"Maybe you should jump straight to the chapter on bulimia."

Missy laughs with an energy the joke doesn't warrant, and an expressive twist of her head sends the tip of her black ponytail wisping across my cheek. This desperate, big-nosed woman with the false vigor of someone on recreational drugs, persisting in her girl's hairdo—I yearn for her every time she rustles past in windsuit and cross-trainers. There is nothing to be gained from imagining what it would be like to perform cunnilingus on her, but that's what I am doing when Herbie St. Germain weaves forward through a gauntlet of orange and brown chairs and obtrudes himself into my personal space.

"Are you tutoring?"

If Herbie were one of my Honors seniors, I might make a nerdy joke based on his verb tense, but Herbie is an eighth grader, and a very slow one. Dimwittedness has made him as sneaky and feckless as an abused dog, he is a farter and a laugher at farts, an eater of inedible substances, a child who is already dismally failing my class, and experience tells me that he will not graduate from Perpetual Succor. I am thinking about how much of my job is spent on lost causes as I clap him on the shoulder and say, "Absolutely, young man."

As he gets a head start toward my room, all the things I am thinking about get twisted in my head, and I say, "These kids are going to be great at oral sex."

"Oh, my God!" Missy stage-whispers, enjoying the fiction that we might be overheard in the booming cafeteria.

"They get so much practice. They can do things with their mouths that my generation only dreamed of."

Missy's helpless giggle confirms my role as roué.

"In the future, the fattest kids will be the most desired partners." The cafeteria is foggy with the frankincense of fried starch. "Somewhere in Georgia or Tennessee there's already a thousand-pound girl who can make boys come just by pursing her lips."

WHEN I WAS YOUNG, I pictured myself dying before I had to choose a career. If that sounds like the cheap self-melancholy of youth, it's not; it's just that when I was thirteen and huffing chemicals from Ziploc bags, the adult world appeared so inscrutable that I could not imagine it holding a place for me—I supposed I would become a hobo or a convict or one of the other icons of failed adulthood whose uniforms children don on Halloween. I liked heavy metal music of terminal hate, adventure-based video games set in worlds of daft magic, serial masturbation, playing with fire, hosting basketball tournaments in my driveway where calling a foul was against the rules, and making amateur films in which everyone—*everyone*—dies at the end, none of which seemed to equip me for leaving the house with a lunchbox every morning at 6:00 like my father or sorting coupons into color-coded boxes like my mother. When our teachers asked us what we wanted to be, I always said President of the United States because it rendered the teachers soft and warbly and gave me a chance to shoot a retard's grimace at the rest of the class for laughs. The less youth I had left, the more aggressively I practiced it. I kept marijuana in my car, in both pockets, in my locker, and in three of my seven classes. I invented *-isms* for my inchoate hatreds, developing the catchphrases of a dickhead philosophy. My teachers I did not so much dislike as ignore, and I was cruel only to the ones who took their jobs seriously. Some secret striver in me apparently dropped a college application in the mail; I taught that little suck-up a lesson by writing excellent papers but turning them in weeks late, daring professors to fail me, by emitting a rank undergraduate odor and cultivating a hell's goatee. I likened any authority figure who demanded something definite of me to a Nazi taskmaster, which makes it rich and remarkable, one of life's mysteries, that I am now standing with a clipboard at the head of a column of students, checking them off as they file toward me with looks of vacant submission and their shoes and socks in hand.

"Hendry." At Perpetual Succor, the students' names are embroidered just above their breast pockets. "Ingargiola."

Behind a partition to my left waits a bioelectrical impedance machine, a sinister little device with two chilly footpads that sends a mild electrical pulse coursing into one leg and collects it from the other, then chatters out a small receipt that subdivides the body's contents into muscle, fat, bone, and water weight, each labeled according to its percentage of the whole. Also waiting behind the partition is Mallory Holland, my student worker, a senior volleyball player with no sympathy for the obese. Mallory skims and files the receipts with the brusque disdain of a traffic court clerk. The impedance machine makes obsolete the use of manual calipers for body-fat testing, but I know Mallory would be perfectly comfortable snatching up a rough handful of flesh and crushing it with a pre-digital instrument.

The public imagines teaching to be a profession of the mind, but in truth it is primarily a profession of the body, and herding students toward ritual humiliation is teaching in its purest form.

"Unferth. Zinsser."

Yet it is also a profession of the mind. Mallory, whom I overhear whispering, *Shut up and stand on the thing,* has just earned a 92 on an essay about Flannery O'Connor in my English V class, though she doesn't know it yet. A 92 is a B+, a good grade for Mallory. She brought me three rough drafts and turned in an essay of depth and clarity entitled "O'Connor's American Gothic," and the well-being I feel as I anticipate her happiness is pure and sustained, and I can feel myself suppressing a smile as I check off the remaining names.

"Forty-one point-something," Mallory says. We're in the hall now, pushing through the noisy crush of students on their way to fifth period. Because Perpetual Succor enrolls five hundred students in a facility built for three hundred, Mallory has to walk behind me with the machine as I forge a path through overstuffed backpacks and the informal postal system of notes thrust from hand to hand. We are conversing in muted yells.

"Not even close to the record," I say. We are talking about Zinsser's body fat. "But he has potential. With the proper regimen, I think we could groom him into a champion."

"Like, protein shakes?"

"Lardsicles. A sugar I.V. during class."

"Sorry," she shouts as she steps on my heel.

I glower at a sophomore with whom I share a running joke that we're always one false move from beating each other up.

"But this hall is full of champions!" I exclaim, and a girl I taught last year smiles sweetly at me from a doorway.

Back in my office, Mallory hands me the receipts, and I slip them into a 3 × 5 hardshell case. With students like Mallory, I feel an imperative to be more interesting than her coaches, to make attractive, by all means fair or foul, the alternative I have in mind for her brain and soul; and this explains why I let her hang around in my office for a few minutes before I send her to her next class, and why, away from the antic flurry of the hallway, I speak to her with a directness I know from experience will flatter her.

"The time we spend on this is entirely wasted," I say in a just-so-you-know tone.

"It's part of my work-study hours," she shrugs.

"Very pragmatic. That'll save you from cynicism."

"Are you turning cynical?"

I talk about the dead-end of cynicism in my English V class. She's doing her best to challenge me, which is cute.

"Only about things with capital letters. The Healthy Children Act. The Patriot Act. No Child Left Behind." The reluctant creak of my office chair might be the doors of thought creaking open and shut in my mind. "I mean, do you really think we're helping Zinsser? The Zinssers of the world?"

"It doesn't feel like it."

"Good," I say, meaning that she is right to trust her feeling. Then something comes together in my head, and I spit it out: "A wealthy country is never going to be thin not because food is cheap but because money erases memory. That's the main thing money does, erases the past."

"People forget what they eat?" she ventures, seeing that I've gotten hung up.

"More like what they know about what they eat. And that there's such a thing as death." The neat nexus of ideas unravels a bit in my brain. "It's the past and future where death is. Eating is always the present."

We sit thinking for a few seconds in my tiny office with its shelves of moribund binders.

"Do you want to forget that I have to go to Calculus?" she asks.

"Ick," I say consolingly as I pull out a pad of passes. I begin to fill the blanks with my red pen. "Speaking of forgetting, there was someone I was going to tell that she had written a great essay and gotten a 92. . . ." I let my brow go distracted and quizzical.

"Are you serious?" Her face breaks open and radiates a satisfaction that we enjoy together. We are beaming at one another across the desk. "Omigod!"

"You've become a really good writer, Mallory." I hand her the pass. "I'm proud to be your teacher."

WORDS ARE THE TOOLS of my work. I am awash in words from bell to bell—or, rather, I wash myself in them and make them my element. As an English teacher, I interpret literary words, I purvey rules governing the use of words, and I grade the words of others. But I also know which words to choose when I speak to a student I've seen cheating if I want her to weep with remorse and which words to use to blunt her remorse just enough to make its cut sweet. I know how to still the mutinous rage that accompanies the return of poor essays by apologizing to the students for having failed to inspire their best work, transmuting their anger into regret that they haven't met my expectations. The words I need to persuade the Quiz Bowl team to work a Saturday-morning car wash leap readily to my mouth. I can be glib in the extreme in the service of a greater cause. At the end of class, my neck and cheeks are often aglow with the after-heat of speech, as if I am no more than a voice organ humming in space, and I often sense that, as an indistinctly shaped man, I barely register as a physical presence to my students. Words are, finally, the only difference between a teacher like me, whose students sit attentively through a lesson, and a teacher like Stephanie Cable, whose students can be heard three rooms away shouting out personal questions about her love life.

This is why it surprises me when Stephanie leans across the library table where we're grading and whispers, "I heard you called Lori Carter fat."

"False."

"She burst into tears, is the story."

"Doubly false."

This rumor annoys me less because of its blatant untruth than because I pride myself on not suffering the gossip that corrodes other teachers' reputations, the anonymous notes to administration, the summer phone calls from parents demanding that their children be scheduled to other sections. I like Stephanie personally because she has learned that I prize feistiness and she does her best to provide it, but professionally she is a shambles, a magnet for huge energies of conflict. Because a bad teacher's every misstep becomes part of public discourse, I know that Stephanie is a high-decibel screamer, an insulter of intelligence (often tempting, never productive), a blamer of personal errors on errors in the textbook, an inadvertent classroom swearer, and a consecutive-day pants-wearer.

"Story is, she went to Mr. J."

"How fascinating."

I might pass by the front office and see whether Johansen's secretary acts funny around me, but I have to finish a quiz about prepositions, and after that I make a few quick changes to my PowerPoint about the Greek theater for English V, and all thoughts of Lori Carter scatter into the incoherent whirlwind that make up a teacher's life.

I AM NOT UNUSED to being a symbol. I have, for some time, been the Aging Bachelor Who Has Given His Life to the School. (I hear the pity and admiration warring in the greetings of students who see me eating dinner alone in the cafeteria-style restaurant across the street from campus.) I am also Really Hard Teacher You Have to Survive to Graduate (my grades are in fact usually too high) and Secret Tested Genius (untrue but amusing). But becoming the liaison for the Healthy Children Act has nationalized my symbolism: when I walk into the faculty lunch room now, I represent an American anxiety more intimate than weapons of mass destruction or gay marriage, an anxiety they put in their mouths three times a day. But the symbolism is mutual. Most of my colleagues' food choices represent to me the stupidity, greed, and waste of our nation, and the faculty lunchroom tends to fan my intolerance for humanity, the pilot light of which is always burning in the crawlspace of my soul.

"Oh, no, there's Wilkins. What you got today, Wilkins, a bran muffin?"

This is Jason Pete, the assistant basketball coach and Earth Science teacher, a person I like everywhere except at the lunch table. He is unable to withhold comment about what I eat because I am the voice of his conscience and he is trying to drown me out. There are a dozen people of various ages and sensibilities at the table, but I say, without the hesitation of someone whom a twenty-year tenure has not coated with infallibility, "You want it? You sound constipated."

Jason giggles the kind of giggle you giggle at a curiosity, a giggle meant to marshal support from the others at the table, and I can tell it has worked even though I am washing my hands at the sink, with my back to him. "What's the matter, Wilkins, your iceberg lettuce didn't tide you over from breakfast?"

"Iceberg lettuce," I say, taking the chair at the opposite end of the long table, "is a non-food for people who like to lie to themselves about nutrition." I know full well that there are, between us, five or six people eating the iceberg lettuce of our cafeteria's salad bar. Two older women, counselors, adopt the special silence of disapproval, though they would never in a million years express this disapproval aloud or even dare to rise and leave in wordless censure. The floor is mine and Jason's. "And what are you eating, Jason?"

"This, this is food. This is a hamburger," he says slowly, pointing. "And these are french fries."

"Don't worry," I say, seeing several other teachers with fast-food bags, "one of these days you'll get to grow up and eat big-boy food."

"Which would be what? *Figs?*" I'd brought dried figs to school about six months earlier, and since he had never seen them before, they'd stuck in his mind and still popped up to frighten him from time to time.

"Oh, you know, just any food consistent with your intelligence," I say trippingly, peeling a banana. "Food with actual nutrients that sustains rather than ravages your body. Food that doesn't destroy the earth that you hypocritically teach a unit about preserving." I nip off the banana tip and speak through it. "That kind of food."

I am prepared to elucidate my points, addressing the carbon-spewing, unsanitary production of the beef in his hamburger, the distant manufacture and flash-freezing of his fries, the unnecessarily large portions he is struggling to finish, the shameful waste of the packaging and of the Styrofoam trays of those with cafeteria food, but a moment's silence tells me they consider my tone uncouth, so I finish my banana in the peace I have created for myself.

"You ever get tired of being grumpy?" Jason asks.

I grin to indicate that he will be allowed to keep his red herring but that he won't enjoy it.

"It keeps me young, Coach."

THE NEXT DAY is a Mass day, and these are the mornings I like our school best, when the students' red-and-blue ties sharpen the halls with rigorous optimism. The ties of the ninth-grade boys, many of whom are still midgets, dangle past their crotches, and the boys wear looks of mild helplessness to inoculate themselves against embarrassment. The girls' ties are square-bottomed and made of the same plaid as their skirts, and the girls look so wholesome and proper that I wish every one of them were my daughter. A teacher two doors down is gently reshaping the knot at Herbie St. Germain's neck.

The Mass itself usually cures me of my innocent cheer. Our chaplain, Father Hank, is a lackluster half-wit whose homilies are characterized by long pauses of forgetfulness, caesurae of five seconds, ten seconds, during which we listen to his amplified breathing and count the volleyballs stuck among the overhead ducts. Then Father Hank performs his magic cookery, intoning the recipe and crumbling ingredients into his golden mixing cup, and I direct the students forward in single file to receive their snack.

Doug Johansen works through the communion line, taking his wafer old-school style, eyes closed and tongue out, then drifts over to me and whispers, "Would you mind talking with Mrs. Carter for a few minutes after school?"

"Not at all."

Doug Johansen is a man so tall that his body defeats all trousers' attempts to cover his ankles, and this is the detail students have latched onto as a shortcut to his personality.

"She has a concern."

I try to read his tone, but the whisper makes it difficult. Doug is one of my oldest friends, a person with whom I have been kicked out of bars, argued about literature, gotten to the bottom of stink bombs and petty harassment, and knelt to unjam the copy machine a thousand times in the last fifteen years. But as the assistant principal, he is also the person who assigns me the extra-contractual tasks that invade my personal life and who, in his efforts to please and imitate our principal, has a workplace insincerity unrivaled in my experience for its opacity and ability to irk. I would like to get one more sentence out of him, but any further comment on my part will reveal a weakness, and I let him drift back into the general stupor. Father Hank does the dishes, caps the leftovers, and blesses us back to class.

AT LUNCH, I help Joe Bergeron with his essay on "What Does it Mean to Be an American?," and I learn that *An American obeys all laws and they don't disagree with the government even when it is wrong.* In sixth period I teach the scene in *Othello* in which Iago explains that, to obtain love, one needs only put money in one's purse. In the narrow passage leading to the faculty lavatories, I bump into Missy Heaton, and we trade lascivious innuendoes about a sexual encounter in the bathroom as we sidle past on our errands. My armpits, in the mirror, are dry, and I have no foreign matter on my face. I have watched myself age in this mirror, and I am trying to convince myself that I have done a good job of it as the bell rings to end the day.

Doug Johansen, Mrs. Carter, and Lori are waiting for me in the conference room, but so are the principal, Bill McGee, and Lori's counselor, Claire LeBlanc, who doubles as the school's lawyer, and I adjust my mood to the proper institutional seriousness. The silence that builds as I choose a seat, pull it up behind me, lay my grade book on the table, and give two clicks to my mechanical pencil might be construed as ominous or intimidating to an observer, but it is actually a courtesy on the part of Doug and Bill. They are waiting for me to signal my readiness by reaching across the narrow oval table, which I do now, and shaking Mrs. Carter's hand with a disarming smile: "Nice to see you, Mrs. Carter. Thanks for coming."

"Mr. Wilkins," Bill begins, "we just want to shed some light on an incident that has caused Lori concern. I'm sure there's been some kind of misunderstanding that you can clear up for us, but Lori says that she was singled out individually in your class, by you and in front of her peers, with a reference to her weight."

"No one has a right to call my daughter fat," Mrs. Carter lunges, her voice steeled with the edge of someone who's been sharpening and resharpening a sentence for hours.

Mrs. Carter is exactly what I think of when I think of the mothers of our school: a wrecked, horrific version of her daughter. Her face, like Lori's, was probably once a face that well-meaning people described as *pretty*, but her efforts to preserve it have become as garish and ineffectual as a mortician's. She is, by any objective measure, morbidly obese.

"Certainly not, Mrs. Carter," Bill says calmly. "I'm sure we can straighten this out to your satisfaction. Mr. Wilkins, do you remember anything you might have said in homeroom that could have made Lori uncomfortable?"

Bill is using the voice he uses for parents, a rationalist Muzak full of easy listening, and I borrow it to say, "Channel One was doing a segment on teen obesity." I put on my I'm-only-guessing-here expression. "Perhaps she was made uncomfortable by that."

"Is it possible that you commented on the segment?"

"I don't think so."

"Is it possible," Doug Johansen bludgeons crudely, bruising the civil tone of the meeting, "that you said, 'Certain people in this room ought to be paying attention instead of smelling their Wite-Out'?"

It crosses my mind to wonder whether Mrs. Carter owns a business that contributes to Perpetual Succor or whether she wields any sort of social clout, but I happen to know that she lives in a trailer and works in a video store. Experience tells me that I can pit my worth to the school against Lori's tuition money and win, but I decide that the notepad in front of Claire LeBlanc recommends a less direct approach.

"No. That did not happen," I say simply, but for the first time I sense a curious lightness on my side of the scales. "I may have requested the attention of the class, but I did not, and would never, embarrass an individual student by reference to Wite-Out or any other item in his or her hand."

"Did you make eye contact with Lori?" Doug asks.

"I make eye contact with all my students."

"But do you see," he continues tiresomely, "how Lori might have felt picked on or singled out by that?"

I pause and look at Doug to let him know how unbecoming his treachery is. I allow a wisp of humor to cross my face in lieu of the truthful remarks I might make at this moment, none of which, it is clear, anyone at this meeting is interested in hearing. I consider letting my faint smile stand as my response, but so that Ms. LeBlanc will have something to record on her notepad, I say, "If Lori felt singled out, I have to say I think it was something to do with her, not me. Something she imagined."

"Well, the problem we have here," Doug says, pressing forward unbelievably, "is that other students heard the comment," and he gestures toward a potted tree in my blind spot, whose shade, I now notice, obscures a sheepishly immobile Mallory Holland. She is trying to make her long body disappear by casting her eyes away from it, toward a corner.

"Mallory," Bill McGee asks, swooping in to deliver the death blow, "did you hear Mr. Wilkins make an individual reference to Lori as having to do with her weight?"

The long moments of reflection during which Mallory might test the truth of her memory and struggle to respond accurately have occurred earlier, I know, in an offstage conversation, so there is no pause now before she says, "Yes."

Mallory Holland can, without irony, be described as Amazonian; Doug Johansen holds a position of legendary thinness in the lore of our school; Bill McGee is a former college tennis player who still stalks the halls with an athlete's nimble grandeur; but instead of the anger I might feel as I look around the table, I can muster only sadness for the way these once-proud souls have been tamed and bested. Claire LeBlanc's pen is waiting for the only thing that can save us from the embarrassment blanketing the room like a black biblical pall—my apology—and I deliver it cheerily and without stint. Among the many skills I have learned in the last twenty years is the ability to balance an apology on the cusp of the moment so that it has no relation to the past or future, but teeters there long enough for everyone to get out of the room.

THAT WAS YESTERDAY. Today I am back in the gym with the impedance machine, and it is, naturally, Lori Carter's period. Mallory swabs the footpad with a vinegar towelette, and Lori steps up. Her feet are doughy and under extreme pressure from above, and I kneel before them to scan the numbers: at 5' 3", she weighs 202 pounds and has 48% body fat. Mallory collects the printout, Lori tugs her socks back on, and the Healthy Children Act, like the Healthy Forests Act and the Clean Skies Act, is revealed as another piece of community theater written by industry and performed by citizen-actors.

I teach the *Inferno* in last period, my usual vigor bled away into a beau-

tiful afternoon light. On my way out of the classroom I bump, literally, into
Missy Heaton.

"I always knew you wanted to throw me down and take me in the
middle of the hall."

"Any day now," I say unconvincingly. "Prepare yourself."

There are no secrets in a school, so we both know Missy is trying to
cheer me up, and we both know why, when she says, in the urgent impera-
tives of a pep captain, "All right, then, right now. Let's go. In front of all
these people."

"At least you'd be physically fit enough to survive my onslaught," I say,
and we smile off down the hall in the warmth of our silly compliments,
though mine isn't entirely genuine. Because the strange truth is, I prefer
fat women. When you are, like me, a man whose life is full of stony concerns and stony words, you don't seek a stony refuge. You seek something
soft you can sink away into. I jot wry notes to chubby spinsters at educational conferences, I lay a caring hand on the plump wrist of a divorced
mother on parent–teacher night, and these are women who both appreciate my regard for their fallen bodies and have no need for larger declara-
tions when I follow them home to bed. The day of rail-thin spinsters is
thankfully gone. Even the word *spinster* doesn't fit its function anymore:
its stingy morphemes belong to sharp elbows in cardigans, unpainted gray
lips, thighs whittled down by years of squeezing them together. My own
marrying years came and went in homeroom competitions and Christmas
dances. But I have been given much in return, and I find all the comfort I
need in the generous hips of our modern spinsters, in the food of their bodies, in the moment when words end and I close my eyes and eat.

OR

THAT WAS THE YEAR I noticed that none of my friends could make a decision.

"There's always Chinese," my wife Margie said, ruining the idea of Chinese by presenting it as a default option whose choice would mean our wills had been too weak to name their true desire.

"Do y'all like Thai?" August asked in a vaguely doubtful way that disowned the suggestion as he made it.

"They do interesting things with bananas."

"Really? Bananas?"

This was August's wife Nancy, who, despite her WASP-y name, was from Medellín and had been kidnapped by the FARC as a child. Either her black-brown eyes or her accent, her worldliness or unworldliness, had intimidated me at first, but then I realized how undiscriminating she was—everything was interesting or funny to her—and I developed a falsely assured way of conducting myself around her that always made me feel a little embarrassed in retrospect.

"Or plantains. Anyway, a dessert thing with ice cream."

"There's always Vietnamese," Margie said, debasing another national cuisine. She was capturing her hair up for departure with a deft twist and tuck.

"I always feel like I've overeaten at Kokapelli's," I said, nixing a burrito place of monstrous portions.

"If the Mona's across the street from Kokapelli's had hummus as good as the Mona's on Banks Street," Margie said, "I could definitely go for Mona's."

"Have they changed their pita?" I asked. "The last time I was there, it seemed like they'd changed the pita."

"I'm actually cool with anything, y'all," August said, and I decided it was OK to hate him a little.

"What are we actually hungry *for*?" Nancy asked.

"Not Italian," Margie said.

"And I'm saying no to po-boys," I said, fanning myself limply in the humidity that was already weighing us down in mid-April. Margie and I had just been debating about whether or not to turn on the air conditioning, which was where the idea of eating out had come from in the first place, which is why we had called August and Nancy. Experience told me that none of us was jockeying for a favorite restaurant; no one was vetoing the preferences of others as an arbitrary exercise of power; none of us would have defended our vetoes if challenged; we simply *could not decide.*

"We're off dairy again," August added as an afterthought, and now I was in a very bad mood indeed. Hunger had painted a thin, vicious glare over the colors of the world, making it look the way I imagined it looking to pit bulls and hornets.

Margie raised her eyebrows at August's comment with what I hoped was hollow politeness, and Nancy bent beneath eye level to intimate, at full volume, "Girl, I've been cheating."

"It's the BGH you have to worry about, not just the dairy per se," Margie said as my humanity baked down into a weaponized mass.

"BGH?"

"Bovine growth hormone, girl," Margie said, borrowing a quirk of speech she would have never used with anyone but Nancy.

Was this conversation unusual? It was not. Margie and I had it several times a week, not only about what to eat but also about whether we should continue our newspaper subscription since it usually went straight from front porch to recycling bin; about whether we could in good conscience forgo news of the war on the *Jim Lehrer NewsHour* in favor of *American Idol;* about whether it was right to let our seventeen-year-old cat's haywire thyroid waste her further or whether we should put her down; and about whether it was time to leave New Orleans for a city of greater sanity, an idea we had been tossing around for years. We excelled at the sophistry of bringing our dissatisfaction with current conditions into exact balance with our distaste for the options. The thing was that not deciding didn't hurt enough to make deciding necessary.

At great violence to my spirit, then, as if dragging myself forth into harsh light, I took out my keys and said:

"I will be having sushi. Even though Kyoto is only five blocks away, I am driving rather than walking, I am ordering a Kirin and a sashimi appetizer, and I'm having that special roll with the green sauce. I'm paying with Discover because I get cash back, and you are invited to join me."

"Gordon," Nancy cooed agreeably, "that sounds perfect."

"Gordon is a genius," August said. "No wonder we stole Charlotte's basketball team."

This was a reference to my job with the New Orleans Sports Commission, a position that involved providing reports about the Commission's financial activities to the state legislature, not committing acts of atrocity and predation with martinis in my hand, as August liked to imagine. It was a job I'd backed into after doing an internship at the Commission during the summer I finished my MBA at Tulane; I'd held the job for ten years now. I did sometimes get free tickets.

"I refused to take no for an answer," I said. "Also I had to fuck a few people."

"Oh, jeez," Margie said, turning for the door.

Nancy spent half of dinner complaining about the tenant they were going to evict because he'd gotten a dog even though the lease expressly forbade it, but I didn't listen too carefully because I knew the eviction wouldn't happen. Talking about the eviction and imagining what the tenant's *stupid ass* would say when he received notice would take the place of the eviction itself, and I spent these moments instead wondering when so much of Margie's hair had turned gray and deciding I liked it. I once had a friend who had his girlfriends wear wigs during sex, and although the comparison was crude, I realized that my wife was continually becoming a new person, and I was interested to meet the people she would become. Margie's face, unlike Nancy's, had common sense and sturdiness, and, unlike Nancy, she didn't keep a less inspiring version of herself hidden beneath makeup. Margie's was a face that could have steered a stagecoach into the setting sun or worn the goggles of a welder or chemist.

"It's in boldface. It's the very first rule."

"I'll give her notice tomorrow, Babe."

"You don't have a choice," I said. But, of course, the moral high ground is always in not choosing. Not choosing allows you to cry foul when circumstances are forced upon you, one of life's most luxurious feelings. Or maybe the climate was just leaching us of motivation. I knew that was the problem for Stephanie and Lila because they often said so, though I think they used *climate* as shorthand for the food and booze and painless music and unpunished ineptitude and general gorgeousness that seep into a person in New Orleans and prevent her from beginning the exercise program she has been planning to begin for years (Stephanie) or from finishing the classes she enrolls in each semester (Lila).

Stephanie flung open the door and bear-clapped first Margie and then me into her plushness.

"You guys always match," she said, looking us over, an assertion that was patently false. "I *love* that."

Lila was slumped among couch cushions watching a replay of the President's announcement that we would soon be incinerating far-off peoples, and her eyes swiveled to touch us in a grim and soundless greeting. Lila took injustice of every type and at whatever distance personally, which is to say she was twenty-two and that her inner sense of things wasn't as blasted as ours, and I respected her right to despondency by settling onto the other end of the couch and quietly considering the remnants of a 9:00 A.M. joint someone had left on the coffee table. I don't smoke pot myself, but I enjoy knowing that others do. Like Stephanie's greasy hair and perpetual baseball cap, their marijuana use represented a relinquishing of claims on society. Having chosen one another, Stephanie and Lila had demanded nothing else from the world in their five years together than to be left alone with the courage of their decision, to consider, foster, and defend it. Lila worked at a daycare center, herding toddlers against her knees; Stephanie tended bar. We had come over so that Margie, who is a high school English teacher, could edit an essay Stephanie had written for the Speyside Sealand Colony, a summer retreat in British Columbia where, for six weeks, to aid the process of self-discovery, the participants were not allowed to speak.

I listened to Stephanie's voice bounding off kitchen surfaces and to President Bush using the word *freedom* with dumb abandon, and I added my patient immobility to Lila's. Lila was the prettier, smarter, and more reserved of the two, and I felt a closer connection to her; Stephanie, I knew, would make it with or without the special support of my friendship. Allowing myself to imagine that Margie's hair had once been the same fine blonde as Lila's led me to the idea that we might both feel better if I laid Lila's head against my shoulder, that I would have wanted somebody to do that for Margie, but I didn't know how to execute the gesture. As I watched our President squint through his text, it occurred to me that making a decision—to drop bombs, say—might just mean you were too stupid to understand a situation in all its paralyzing complexity.

"Turn this depressing shit *off*!" Stephanie exclaimed a bit later, capering in and swiping the remote off the table.

"I was just getting that tickly patriotic feeling," I said as static tingled around the snuffed TV. "How was it?" I asked Margie, meaning Stephanie's essay.

"It was awesome. Did you know this person made a pilgrimage to see Sai Baba?"

Part of why you never thought of Stephanie as fat, although she was obviously overweight, was that she still employed her body the way she had when she was an all-state softball player in California, in quick, agile bursts that were physical analogues of *Hum-babe, hum-babe, it's you, it's you, no-batter, you-got-her, you-got-her, you-got-her, SWING,* and it was her volubility of body and speech I had in mind when I said, "Maybe they have a sister camp where you aren't allowed to *stop* talking."

"I know, it's fucked up," she said with a smile of delight, "but I'm into it. Lila's been giving me the silent treatment to get me ready."

Lila, observing us with steadfast, blinkless blue eyes, wasn't to be drawn out of her bleak resolve, any more than Stephanie was to be drawn, by Lila's bleakness, out of her good humor.

"What are you two doing today?" Stephanie asked.

"We may go look at couches. We've got a situation in the living room."

"Yeah, me too," she stage-whispered, but Lila kept her own counsel. We bowed out.

But neither of us, we agreed in the car, wanted to put ourselves through the suburban nightmare of the furniture store, so instead of performing the industrious acts of improvement I had charted out for myself during the week, I settled into Fox Saturday Baseball, and Margie graded essays. Every so often she brought one out to me.

"*I feel that curfews for a kid is wrong if they are of reasonable age,*" she read, standing directly in front of the TV. I muted the game and looked at her because I had reached a point in my life where I understood sports not as a thing in itself requiring total attention, but as a running curiosity I could check into and out of at any time without danger of losing crucial information. "*Curfews is coming in early instead of you want to come in late.*"

"From the mouths of babes," I said, assuming these were her ninth graders, not the Honors seniors she taught. "How many of those do you have?"

"Fifty," she said, rolling her eyes and performing a military about-face before marching off to her duty. But there's nothing Margie likes better than a fat stack of essays she can wade into with a green pen, righting errors and appending an encouraging statement in jaunty cursive.

St. Louis had just put the leadoff man on in the sixth, and their pitcher was now at the plate with Houston ahead by two runs. There ensued one of those episodes of complex deliberation, marked by throws to first and step-offs and visits to the mound, which casual observers of baseball find so intolerable because there is an impression of nothing happening, but which former players know as the fullest moments of the sport, humming with variables and subtle adjustments. (I was a catcher in high school.) There are as many ways to defend a bunt as there are hunches, scouting reports, and superstitions about the opponent's tendencies, but almost all of them involve a flurry of infielders to unaccustomed places on the field, a treacherous, commonplace choreography requiring five or six people to react correctly at once, each sprinting to a vacated area. It was a play whose effects, ill or good, would ripple forward through the rest of the game.

But on the first pitch—a ball, high—the batter did not square around. Houston's first baseman, the player most likely to take a line-drive off the forehead if the batter swung away, glanced into his dugout. I knew he would be told to charge the plate again, on the assumption that the batter, having performed a fake to disquiet the defense, would now bunt obediently, as statistics demanded. But on the second pitch, the batter squared halfway and then pulled back in mid-delivery for a check swing that sent the first baseman backpedaling madly. Ball two.

Geographically, I should have been rooting for Houston. But Houston had taken several of our friends from us, it was a faceless, efficient anti-New Orleans in love with the future, and there was nothing I liked about it, so I was pulling for St. Louis.

"*Since we both been through so much together,*" Margie yelled from the next room, "*I'm sure we can achieve another unbreakable ambition.*"

"Oh, shit," I yelled back, in a proper tone of dismay over the blithe ignorance of America's youth as the batter bunted the third pitch foul. It was only one pitch, but it restored all the variables of the situation and tipped the weakness of the Cardinals' hand. I understood the advantage of saving their pitcher for the next inning, but sending him to the plate was tantamount to conceding the chance of a big rally. The first baseman was moving in confidently now, with hungry steps, and the other fielders were shading toward the spots they would occupy when the bunt went down, when the runner at first did something unexpected by breaking toward second at full speed.

The difference between what the runner did and what he was supposed to do—wait for the bunt to hit the grass before committing to second—was infinitesimal, but it was enough to trigger the fielders' instincts not for a bunt, but for a steal. The second baseman hesitated on his way to first, the pitcher threw a pitch over the outer part of the plate to give his catcher a better ball to handle, and the batter, thinking to protect the runner by sweeping the bat through the catcher's workspace, cued a cheap blooper that splatted down directly atop the abandoned first-base bag and spun off into shallow right field. It was a beautiful baseball play, whimsical, unmerited, and totally subject to chance. I assumed that somebody had missed a sign.

Margie came in and stood in front of the TV. I muted it.

"I can't take it, Gordon," she said. She had a mustache of perspiration.

"No problem," I said, and we went through the house shutting the windows and doors.

WHAT WAS AT STAKE for any of us? Only the texture of the way we lived. In our jobs we were models of decisiveness—Margie shaped a hundred futures a day with detentions and seating charts, I signed off on the correct treatment of tens of millions of dollars, Stephanie chastised or rewarded the patrons at her bar with queenly rigor, and August was an engineer at Murphy Oil, responsible for the safety of thousands—but nothing outside our jobs, in what might be called our *lives*, equipped us to act with confidence, and I think we felt that we were stand-ins in roles intended for more substantial people. So I placed large numbers in small boxes and learned with dismay from an entertainment website that my *American Idol* favorite, Trenyce, had a felony arrest on her record, and I emailed Margie about this, and then I entered our personal figures at a mortgage refinancing site to weigh the benefits before skimming the text of Osama bin Laden's latest video and reaching over the carpeted wall of my cubicle to shake hands with Paul Silas, coach of the Hornets, who none of us knew would soon be fired. I learned that *SI* had posted advance shots from its Swimsuit Issue because Gavin Wheeler had emailed me the link, and I knew he wanted my opinion because before I could even get past *SI*'s masthead screen, Gavin had jogged across the room to hover at my shoulder.

"Gordon," he said, "I know a brother is supposed to love a big ass, but I got to tell you, I straight-up love titties."

If he wanted to indulge his appreciation for breasts, there were plenty of more suitable destinations on the net, the women in the *SI* shoot being rather modestly endowed, and I told him so.

"I didn't say they had to be big. I just said I loved them."

Gavin and I had been providing checks and balances to the other's idea of beauty since high school, where we were in the same graduating class. I remember Geometry, for example, mostly in terms of the spheres and cones of our female classmates, those shapes we discussed in theoretical terms as if they possessed meaning separate from the larger person. Even then, Gavin's tastes were less ecumenical than mine because, to be honest, they could afford to be—he was startlingly handsome, and everyone knew that his athletic genius would eventually lift him beyond our little school with its button-down shirts and brown loafers, where as a tenth grader he was already getting national attention as a shooting guard. He played college ball at LSU and then spent two years with the Knicks before he blew out his knee. Now he was a lobbyist for the Commission, as well as the guy who took prospective Saints and Hornets to the French Quarter as chairman of the Welcoming Committee. *I know a brother is supposed to love a big ass* is the kind of thing Gavin said to let white people know that he saw race as a humorous accident that he didn't hold against them. In truth, Gavin had never had to make the same kinds of choices about race that most people had; talent and affability had made him colorless.

"These girls are like twelve, Gavin."

"It's a sick world," he laughed with a tinge of helpless insanity, his necktie dangling onto my keyboard. "Sick world, man."

"This looks like a very breathable fabric."

"I like what she's done with those shells."

"I like what she's about to do with those shells."

We paused at a photo of a statuesque redhead, very tall and very pale, amidst twenty or thirty grinning, clowning black boys in a native desert. Some of the boys were out of focus, some had grass or sticks lodged in their webby hair, and two boys at the edge of the frame were wrestling in the dust.

"This is our new ambassador to the Sudan," I said, in an I-don't-know-if-you've-heard-yet tone. "Notice how she's not wearing shoes as a way of fitting in with the culture."

"She gave her outerwear to the relief effort." She wore only the most meager of red bikinis.

"She's a humanitarian."

"But she doesn't do it for the accolades."

Lew Andry came over from his desk. Lew was a wiry sixty-year-old with hair that had gone from brown to gray and gray to yellow, and whose rough exterior hid a rougher interior. I was a little afraid of Lew. He featured an insinuating grin that suggested his core beliefs were deeply dastardly and that when he chose, he could expose them to you and reduce you to ash.

Lew's commentary on the photo largely involved the verb *plummet*, as in which parts of the model he would like to plummet his penis into.

"Show some respect," Gavin said. "This is an American official."

"I'd like to plummet it in her ear."

I saw my own eyebrows rise in reflection along the monitor's upper edge.

Lew provided several more statements for consideration, all involving innovative manipulation of the model's limbs and sensibilities. Gavin might normally have said something like *Look at the brothers all fighting over a white woman*, or *Young lady took a wrong turn and wandered into the projects*, but I knew that he was avoiding such jokes out of courtesy to Lew, and that Lew—whose ideas about black people were, let's say, old-fashioned—was returning the favor. So we settled for the common brutalities that men use in reference to women, and then Gavin and I went to lunch at a burger joint where people kept yelling his name across the room.

"Is Margie still talking about moving?" he asked, dripping Tabasco onto a saltine as we waited for a server.

Margie talked about it, I explained, and then I talked about it; we just didn't talk about it at the same time. We had heard magical tales of cities with infrastructure, cities with functioning public schools and a corporate base, and these tales were beginning to have their effect. Both Atlanta and Houston had come up as possible destinations, and we had at various times monitored the online listings of both newspapers for houses in our range. Margie and I had been astonished and abashed by our visit to a grocery store in Atlanta—its cleanliness, spaciousness, and decency were things we mistrusted, experience having taught us that we didn't deserve them. The cleanness in general of other cities never failed to impress us. I mean, where was their *garbage*? But we also shared a stark horror of ending up in an antiseptic suburb, and we thought of life in New Orleans as the difficult but correct thing to do, as a moral obligation of sorts, like baking from scratch or going to Mass, two more things most of our friends had given up.

A week later we began to carpet-bomb Iraq. Trenyce was eliminated from *American Idol,* which caused me a keen sense of waste and injustice. Television provided the illusion of choice in automobiles, representative government, and the health of our bodies, and then it was summer. Summer in Louisiana, I think, is what explains people like Edwin Edwards and David Duke: while the rest of us mostly try to sit still for four months of the year, a few industrious souls—and perhaps they are lizards—continue slithering through the general stupor with shrewd slit eyes. Admiring their initiative, we allow them to frolic in the mud until the Feds sweep in and make handbags out of them. The rest of us spend those months immobilized between the sinking air and rising water, our vision fogged by mist.

Sometime in July, David and Sophie invited us to a Zephyrs game. The Zephyrs are the Astros' Triple-A baseball team in New Orleans, and on Thursdays the park offers 2-for-1 beer, the mathematics of which is unassailable. By the third inning, I had a soft appreciation for all the smells and colors of the world, by the fifth I felt very close to the punch line of a grand joke, but by the seventh I felt dim and waterlogged, bored with the lukewarm cup in my hand but unable to put it down. It seemed, suddenly, that my life had gone as far as possible in a certain direction.

"I think it's time to leave New Orleans," I said.

Margie kept shelling her peanuts, waiting to see whether she needed to take me seriously.

"Why the hell would you do that, Gordon?" David demanded in the wounded tone of a person whose own life choices would be called into question if Margie and I left. David was a keeper at the zoo, a man often photographed for the newspaper pressure-washing elephants and shouldering pythons, and Sophie, who had gone to get more beer, taught biology at Margie's school. David and Sophie were science-people, the kind who gardened and had tattoos and made their own beer, not the kind who suffered upset stomachs in public. Except for their child and the fact that they were much better looking than we were, they reminded Margie and me of ourselves ten years earlier.

"I don't know," I said, exercising my cruelty, "maybe I'm just growing up. Stupidity isn't as entertaining to me as it once was." Margie and I had learned over the years that we didn't have to inflict harm on each other in conversation, that nothing we believed was quite worth insulting each other about, but when David drank, he thundered through conversations like a bull, and sometimes I couldn't resist unsheathing my little knives. "Everyone in this city is running at about two-thirds power."

"Maybe the other one third of you is a dick," David smiled.

I laid a hand on Margie's damp leg, and we watched someone's kid race the mascot, a seven-foot-tall nutria, around the bases.

"I sometimes picture myself on a treadmill behind a plate-glass window," Margie said, referring to a future moment in the shiny metropolis of our choosing. The nutria took a comic spill.

I said, "I picture myself not rooting for the goddamn Saints." If David's bouncing leg and aggressive attention to the field hadn't already signaled that he was finished with our conversation, this would have finished him. To David, any statement of less than total belief in the Saints was apostasy. "Storm drains that drain. Cops that solve crimes." All of this was so antithetical to my real feelings that it was like punching myself in the gut, which is why I was able to be so cavalier about it.

"Subject-verb agreement," Margie said.

"What is you talking about?" Sophie joked, leaning from the aisle so we could twist our beers from the cardboard tray. As David turned for his, I shot him a middle finger, and he smiled beneath his sunglasses as the first pitch of the inning smacked the mitt.

"Moving out of the city," I said, flattening myself as Sophie passed.

"Yeah, right."

"Is it really so unthinkable?" I asked, and then I heard a sound off the bat that seemed directed in a peculiar way at me, and I looked up to see a foul ball arcing directly toward my head.

The ball seemed an almost stationary object in the air, poised but virulently spinning as it sought me on a line. Then it burst into motion, and I had time only to throw my arms over my face and twist in self-preservation before the ball struck my shoulder and rebounded into the rows behind us.

Being an accident-prone drinker and therefore practiced at gauging the seriousness of my injuries, I knew I was unhurt. I worked the shoulder to prove this to the others, still standing in the cramped aisle, a little off-balance against my up-sprung seat. Margie, her face etched with leftover terror, exclaimed, "Jesus Christ, Gordon," her concern sublimating into annoyance.

David's perfect teeth were laughing at me beneath his sunglasses, and

I was laughing at myself, a knowing cackle, though I couldn't have said what it was I knew. I felt sealed inside the plastic wrap of myself, glisteny and stupid. But I was a master of stupidity. I was a genius at its local forms, highly adapted in dumbness, and I employed it with the simple virtuosity of an athlete employing his limbs. The stupidity of athletes, often decried, is in fact the thing that makes them beautiful. They set their minds aside and achieve the dumb grace that's possible when you realize that your choices have already been made for you.

Kids Make Their Own Houses

I NEVER LOVED HELEN MORE than when she was talking about education.

This is a woman, I tell you, who could use words like *standards* and *benchmarks* with force and clarity, as if they were more than abstract terms handed down by the state. This is a woman who could make you believe no child need be left behind. This is a woman who could run a Smart Board. You may think I am being wry. I am not. To see Helen confidently integrating technology, bending its sleek surfaces to her will with an ease so unlike my own submissive truce with things mechanical—this, to me, was beautiful.

We were rehearsing in her basement.

"Realignment of your curriculum to state norms," she was saying, "is important for many reasons, one being the movement toward accountability we are seeing in the schools. As something to hold up and say, 'Here's the knowledge my students have accomplished.' The second being that in under-resourced districts like yours"—we were to give a seminar in Crowley, Louisiana—"you should experience an immediate and measurable jump in exit test scores."

She saw a cloud flutter across my face.

"What."

"Do we believe that? I don't think I believe that."

"Yes, you do." The coercive optimism of a former cheerleading coach buoyed her words. "Come on."

"I'm thinking the same exhausted teachers are going to be teaching the same unprepared kids in schools with what, chickens running through the cafeteria. I mean."

"Come on, Gerald. You can do it."

This was one of the pep talks I occasionally required. Helen's confidence in what we had done—quitting our teaching jobs, setting ourselves up as educational consultants, destroying her engagement with our affair—never wavered. Mine did. I was a leaky ship wracked by the winds of my own conscience, and she was the steady shore I kept tacking back to.

"Are you sure? *Can* I do it?"

She saw that I was partly playing and cracked a mischievous grin. She hated to waste time but loved to play. She was wearing brown corduroy overalls with a pair of embroidered flowers on the central chest pocket, their stems crossed sentimentally, an atypically girlish choice for her but one I found very affecting.

"If I tell you you can do it, you can do it."

I shook my head with fake doubt, feeling the electricity of the step she took toward me. "I'm not feeling it."

"Bitch," she said, taking another step and planting her hands on her hips, "you're going to believe it because it's what we're saying," and we laughed the dizzy laugh of people for whom everything has become unexpectedly new and fun. Helen and I had worked side by side for fifteen years in the MacKinley County school system, fifteen years of teen pregnancy and bathroom passes and dead-end initiatives and rare human triumph. We had sat on committees where we schemed with and against one another; as sitting members of the Discipline Board, we had scolded, strong-armed, and expelled students; I had passed the doorway of her classroom as she lectured about the Vietnam Era in a headband and fringed vest, props that became oddly touching as she aged. Rumors about the dissolution of her first marriage had trickled down to me, as to everyone else, in the faculty lounge, and, like everyone else, I had tried to detect the signs of devastation in her professional behavior. (There were none.) And then, last January, as heads of our respective departments, we were asked to attend a seminar about raising our school's ACT scores, a seminar about whose substance I was already feeling cynical before we were instructed to draw the animal that best represented our feelings about having to alter our curricula and downright hateful by the time we received our catered lunch of pressed chicken in floury white sauce. I steadied my plastic knife and remarked that *I* could throw irrelevant cartoons onto an overhead projector and peddle test-taking hints in half the time and with twice the verve of the idiots running the seminar. How could these people sleep at night knowing how many irretrievable hours of other people's lives they'd etc., etc. Helen was offended by their lack of organization. We continued the conversation over a cigarette outside, beneath a corrugated awning where the ash urns were. I had a set of essays waiting for me at home in which half the students would compare *The Red Badge of Courage* to one or another movie. We were standing there smoking the smoke of the near-dead, smoking to kill ourselves, when we realized not only that there was an easier way, but that *it was okay for us to take it.* Helen said, "Fuck it, let's do it," and it seemed to me that if Helen Bruno could say it, we could do it. Helen had been Teacher of the Year last year, I had been Teacher of the Year the year before that, and she was engaged to an oil-field manager named Rusty, but we stood there valiantly choosing a future where we would throw all that away for billing rates of four hundred dollars per hour and weekends in climateless hotel rooms with six versions of Showtime. I was wondering if by *it*, she was thinking only of consulting or also of the way we had giggled back from the hotel bar the night before and fooled around on top of the slick bedspread, when she added, "I'm so sick of always having to tell someone where I'm going and how long I'll be there," and waggled her ring hand. I wanted to reciprocate the sentiment and also to signal my approval of a mode of discourse that wouldn't duplicate the evasions and niceties of my own failed marriage, so I said something about how all forms of responsibility are ultimately infantilizing. The way of speaking Helen and I fell upon was only a slightly less guarded form of the backroom speech of all teachers, who say to each other the vaguely shocking things they spend their public lives muting in the name of propriety.

She was halfway across the basement, in the projector's unfocused glow. Helen is not conventionally beautiful, but I liked her physical substance and athleticism. She has the kind of legs you could trust for guidance in a hailstorm or riot. Chastened by half a life's trials, she had aligned her bodily self with the demands of the world and achieved a tempered grace. The word *performance* played in watery capitals across the ridged terrain of her waist as she took the last three steps and grabbed my collar in both hands.

"You think I really believe the schools will ever amount to anything in this shithole state? I don't even care."

It was the sexiest, most godless thing I had ever heard anyone say.

I knelt to untie her clean white running shoes, and we took each other roughly on the basement floor.

BUT THIS ISN'T a story about how bad two people can help each other become. Or it isn't only about that. It's about how you can work with someone for fifteen years, watch her eat twenty-five hundred lunches across a sticky table, stand in line with her at the copy machine as she cuts and pastes maps of the Thirteen Colonies, urge your homeroom to vanquish her homeroom in contests involving tempera paint and butcher paper, and still barely know the first thing about her. It's about the fantastic difficulty of knowing another human, even if you're on a fast-track of revelation and abandon. I sometimes thought of my ex-wife as Helen and I drove to Motel 6's and Super 8's along the American interstate highway system, coordinating my cigarette intake to the mile markers as Helen governed our windswept flight with her left wrist. My wife and I had conspired in a view of marriage as a limited liability agreement requiring both parties to leave inviolate the essential nature of the other by restricting their conversation to dinner plans and the health of pets. In terms of Bloom's taxonomy, my understanding of my wife never moved much past *knowledge,* the level of rote names and dates, and I reminded myself of this every time Helen—in this case just outside Vicksburg, Mississippi— plunged her hand deep into the moist recesses of her soul and pulled out something sick and wriggling.

"Why did it take me so long to realize I hate kids?"

NPR was airing a segment about teens who start their own charities. Helen was at pains, I could see, to locate words that would carry the weight of her feeling, and I waited as a mile's worth of orange construction cones whisked past on the left.

"The falseness of the way you have to interact with them. That whole lie of how you present yourself. Which we do because we have this myth that they're innocent. When the truth is they're selfish and nasty."

Helen's arm on a steering wheel is a firm and purposeful thing, given solidity by years of hefting teacher's editions and emphasizing her points on the board with stunts of chalk. I rooted through the junk drawer of my own heart for a sentiment to match as I watched her arm edge the wheel left, right. I had lied to students, true, lied to them frequently, but they were lies of good cheer and good will, the kind of lies whose maintenance made me a better person and our school a better place. I could be accused of serving up a false joviality that made my students see me as a person with more faith in the future than experience had taught me it was safe to have, but what of that? Was it my place to brutalize them with stories of failed potential, breached trust, lives cut short by unregulated capital? If I was lying when I described the things my students might become in my letters of recommendation to colleges, the artists and missionaries and curers of disease, then these were lies I needed too. Except that I didn't have students anymore. I had given them up, and with them the fleecy untruths we had used to cushion each other's fall through the world, in favor of a missile for two aimed relentlessly at the soft targets of our former lives.

"I guess we should stop telling them that they'll grow an extra arm if they smoke pot," I conceded, "stuff like that. We probably do burn up a certain amount of trust with that kind of lie."

"You totally misunderstood me. I blame the *kids*."

Helen's mouth made what, for lack of a more precise word, would have to be called a smile. We went dancing that night, that simple and exalted thing people in a civilization do, and I kissed her when they played "All of Me." But I am getting ahead of myself.

OUR SCHOOL, the school Helen and I taught at before we leased our souls to a devil's trade, was located in a suburban dell settled and kept tidy by white flight. I mention this because I wouldn't want to suggest that we were war-torn from disarming kids with weapons chiseled in shop class, holding our breaths in bombed-out lavatories. Ours was a school that allowed families who drove Lexuses to speak about the importance of public education while enjoying the peace of mind that came from not having to send their kids to school with the kids of families who drove Hyundais. It was partly my ability to form sentences like this, glinting with shards of cynicism, that convinced me I had to get out.

My principal was surprised. He was a tireless clearinghouse of rumor and information, a man who took pride in never being caught off guard, but I hadn't shown any of the advance signs teachers show when they're preparing to bail out—the stupor, the torpor, the rancor—and the way he tapped a gold pen some niece or nephew had given him against the palm of his left hand told me he was nonplussed.

"This is a complete shock, Gerald. I thought we could count on you to be here at MacKinley South forever." Employing the language of betrayal was one of the ways he got people to do things for him, sit on committees and the like; I recognized it as a valid institutional gambit and didn't hold it against him. "For goodness' sake, you're one of our best teachers. You're what MacKinley South *means* to many of these students."

I can't say whether he was right or not, but I knew that at least part of his consternation came from the thought of having to place an ad in the paper and spend two or three days of his summer interviewing applicants who would show up with Fu Manchu mustaches and vestigial ponytails. I couldn't think of a way to say that I was putting my own needs before the needs of the students for the first time in fifteen years without its sounding so selfish as to seem a personal insult against him, so I settled for something bland and unanswerable like *It's time for me to try something new.* Some other teacher could be what MacKinley South means to the students—although, I reflected, not Helen, because she was coming in fifteen minutes later to tell him the same thing.

COMPARED TO a teacher's life, the life of an educational consultant is criminally easy. I found myself buttering leisurely bagels in the mid-morning glow of Helen's kitchen nook. I reread novels that I hadn't had time to read since graduate school and that I had been recommending to people for twenty years and found I didn't like them anymore; I read with new appreciation books I had spent my life denigrating because my youth had prevented me from having proper sympathy for them. I was growing and improving as a human being. I didn't let dishes sit in the sink overnight anymore. I actually thought consciously about my hair. Two or three days out of seven—though often on Saturdays, it must be admitted—I donned a suit and did my undemanding work, then ate dinners paid for by administrators who wanted to impress me with the progressivism of their districts, essentially decent but harried and needy people. But I've gotten ahead of myself again. Helen and I were still pasting text and formatting slides, assembling the graphs and tables of our nascent trade.

By the time our teaching checks ran out in July, I knew the lobes and fissures of Helen's mind and body well enough to have at least passed a multiple-choice test on the subject. I hardly spent any time at my own house anymore, in part because we were putting in long hours on our presentation and in part because we had agreed to consolidate our resources in the name of thrift. A certain amount of software had to be purchased, a certain amount of hardware. A certain amount of three-ring binders and two-colored highlighters so teachers could annotate the charts we would supply.

To construct even the most vapid of presentations on the most elementary of subjects takes longer than one would suppose, but I enjoyed every minute I spent in that house with its thick evidence of another life. I found a half-empty jarlet of cardamom in Helen's cupboard and a chill ran through me—I can't explain why. A small porcelain figurine of a Siamese cat on her dresser gave me a half-hour's speculation about how long she had owned it and what it might mean to her. The angle of her toaster seemed to suggest whole philosophies of living. Here was a woman who had been alone in her house for five years and built a humid personal atmosphere of rituals and mundana which I could now study in the most intimate of ways. Do you understand what I am saying? I wanted to subsume myself within another human being, disappear into the baseness and beauty of someone in a way which I not only never achieved with my ex-wife, but never even dreamed of. Walking through the rooms of Helen's house, I finally understood my students' fascination with my private life. A teacher is both more and less than fully human, narrowed into the necessities of discipline and subject matter; glimpsing the dandruff shampoo or family photos behind the public figure brings him back into the human family, where you can love or destroy him as you wish.

HELEN TOOK one of my Celebrex, I took one of her Claritin, and we went hiking.

By *hiking* I don't mean humping sixty pounds of specialist gear to a GPS objective; I mean an undemanding stroll in the woods behind her house.

"Helen, would you say I'm a trivial person?"

But she was intent on the leafy incline we had chosen, picking our path upward through thickets of trees whose proper names I didn't know, a million board-feet of inscrutable nature. She wasn't the most attentive conversationalist in any case. I huffed behind her, spacing my footfalls to the smudges her own steps had made in the years-old carpet of leaves.

"I obsess about the angle of staples in documents. I use a single brand of ink pen exclusively."

Her right foot slid out from under her, and I kept her from falling by catching a hand against her lower back. We continued up the rise.

"I need my socks to be an exact height. Isn't there something more to life?" It was the question I meant to ask, but my sense that she was privately laughing at me filled the sentence with ironic pathos as I spoke it, the lament of a TV preacher.

"Look," she said.

At the top of the hill, which I reached with two more steep lunges, the ground fell away into a ravine deep enough to take away what little breath I had left, a plunging green gorge of plant life and whizzing birds watered by a silent rill far below. The classroom transcendentalist in me wants to say there was a mystic fog hanging over the land. In part because I am afraid of heights, and in part because I was humbled by the view, I dropped to one knee and took hold of Helen's calf.

"We used to come here when we were kids," she said.

"It's beautiful. I feel kind of unworthy."

"To smoke and French kiss and whatnot."

"Where did you live then?"

"Where I live now. I've been living in the same house since I was born."

I tried to absorb the meaning of this. The ridge I knelt on had been trodden by Helen at nine, Helen at eleven and fourteen. This very soil— I reached down and rummaged it—held the impress and memory of her tentative middle-school necking and furtive first cigarettes, all her junior-high longings. This is where she had come to map out the life which now included me. I felt overwhelmed by the blunt force of existence, the majesty and briefness of it.

"We used to get down to the water over there," she said, pointing to the shallowest part of the decline, a descent only a teenager flush with his own immortality would attempt. "We built little dams and lit stuff on fire. Playing with fire in the woods," giggling at the recklessness of it; then she took a seat next to me on the loamy precipice.

"I could live here," I said. "I really could."

I don't know whether a sneer can be pretty, as in *She sneered prettily,* but that's what I'm asking you to imagine.

"Let me rephrase. Assuming someone told me which mushrooms not to eat and how to keep birds from pecking my eyes out when I sleep, I think I have the temperament for it. Some sylvan gene deep in my body."

"I wanted to move to Oregon after high school and fight the logging industry. I spent my whole senior year telling everybody I was going to go live on a platform."

I admitted that I had signed up for the Peace Corps after watching *Pather Panchali* but balked at the last second and ended up working in my uncle's construction business.

"Do you regret that?"

We turned to face each other, our legs crossed, kneecaps touching.

"My ex-wife's favorite thing to say is that regret is pointless. Which I think makes a certain sense."

"It makes sense, but not to you."

I rocked forward and planted my hands at the top of her thighs, in the hollows where her legs and hips met. "Let's build a house out of vines and spider webs and live back here, never come out," I proposed.

"Follow me," she said, pushing me away.

She led me left along the ridge, left again, angling back down the hill we had climbed, and then followed a thin, dried-up watercourse choked with leaves that I would never have noticed on my own. After five minutes or so, she hopped down over a small waist-high falls, also dry, into a cove or grotto whose central feature was the exposed root structure of an immense toppled tree. Even on its side, the tree was taller than I was, the airy ganglia of its underside stretching over my head like a frilly awning. The divot left by the yanked roots had been deepened and improved by human hands into a common area that held a cast-off card table, two upturned industrial buckets for seats, and various scattered implements of tinkering and chopping. Having fallen up a hill, the tree's cupped underside provided a tilted half-roof for the hobbit dwelling below.

"I guess kids still come here," she said. The sad shortness of human life pierced me once more, but my purely personal reflection was swept quickly aside by the epiphany that Helen was revealing to me the rebus-puzzle of a childhood of neglect and self-reliance, and that, if I could only solve the puzzle, I would both win and save her.

On the way back to the house, Helen fell and sprained her ankle. I was behind her, and I saw her foot sink into the hidden hole left by some burrowing animal, and I heard her light squeal of surprise and pain as she fell. I rushed to help her, but she was inconsolable—she was sure she had broken it. From where we were, I could almost see the clearing that marked the edge of her property, which heavily informed what I did next: bending down, I lifted her and carried her the few hundred yards back to the house. Several times as I crab-walked through the crowded trees or felt my kneecaps creak and twinge, I thought I would falter. But I found new strength each time by imagining that my ex-wife was watching and by thinking about the things she would say if she were.

BY SEPTEMBER, nostalgia was hitting me hard. I daydreamed of booming tubas at pep rallies in the gym. I remembered with fondness the sweet flurry of uniforms into doorways as the tardy bell rang. I wondered about the academic and social fate of Cash Monet, that student with the most repeatable of names and a crippling case of acne who came to my classroom at lunch every day to discuss the arbitrary cruelty of God. I wanted to know how the English III students with whom I had read Hawthorne and Poe were doing in Mrs. Richardson's English IV class. (Were they constructing specific, arguable thesis statements? Did their body paragraphs begin with clear topic sentences? Were they proofreading carefully, making last-minute corrections in a neat hand with a black pen?) And I wanted to see who had taken my place in their affections. Part of me knew it was a bad idea—Helen told me it was a bad idea—but I convinced her to come to a football game.

People started recognizing us in the half-dark of the parking lot, gaggles of parents hailing us in the crepuscule. I had disliked many of these parents, but I was vaguely offended to see that their lives had continued in my absence, that they were tripping out to sporting events with such blithe unconcern. But it was their unspoiled children I longed to see, and that's who mobbed me—mobbed us, I should say—when we pushed through the turnstile.

"Mr. Wellman! Ms. Bruno!"

They gathered around us in their ill-fitting jeans (too tight on the girls, too loose on the boys) and told us about their grades and their friends, their ambitions and fears. Yvette Harfield, a permanently cowed girl with oily hair from my freshman Study Skills class, fixed me with a deeply needy look—the look that destines certain women to marry men who will mistreat them—and asked if I liked my new job. I said what she wanted me to say, that I missed MacKinley South and missed my students—which was in fact the truth as I said it and is the truth now, as I write it. Michelle Boggs blushed mischievously and asked Helen and me whether the rumors about our relationship were true (someone had seen us together at Winn-Dixie, someone else had seen me spray-washing the car as Helen sat inside behind the streaming windows). I made a joke about Ms. Bruno's preferring taller men, which Michelle, who is 6' 1", found funny. I clapped Tommy Carwell on the shoulder and gestured imperially toward the stands. "Let's go find a seat," I said, "so folks can get through."

MacKinley South was losing 21–0 by halftime, which meant everything was right with the world. The best athletes at MacKinley South don't play football anymore, they play soccer. The same shadow is falling over schools throughout the South, and I find the shift disturbing, though perhaps beneficial to civilization. I want bone-crunching hits at high skill levels. As a man, I want my team to dominate other men's teams mentally and physically. But the students at MacKinley South don't care whether the football team wins or not. Football, for them, is less a sport than a social opportunity, and so I duly record a sample of our conversation:

"We have to compare Edna in *The Awakening* to Hester in *The Scarlet Letter*."

"That's a good assignment. Whose class is this?"

"Miss Hardesky. The new lady."

"That's a great assignment. Why didn't I think of that? Hello, Mr. Morton."

"She's *mean*. She yelled at Mike."

"Scarlotti? I'm sure he deserved it."

"Mr. Wellman!"

"Whoa, now that was a football play."

"I have to go find my sister."

"Peace, love, and happiness. Jason, still kissing teachers' butts for grades?"

"As if. I told Mr. Letort he ought to be more professional and look over the vocabulary words he's teaching before he teaches them. He had no idea how to pronounce *sangfroid*."

"Blame that on the French, not Letort. Hi, Mr. Becker."

"In Mrs. Ellis's class I never take out a book, and I'm making a B. I read stereo equipment catalogs."

"You want me to say I'm proud of you? You're a shyster, and someday you'll bring down the U.S. banking system."

"This team," pointing at the field. "Bunch of pussies. See you later."

"Ciao."

"Mr. Wellman, I'm driving now."

"Now *that* was a football play. Wait, driving? What are you, nine years old?"

"I'm sixteen!"

(I fake-grab my heart, indicating shock at the precipitous march of time and, by implication, at my own dwindling quotient of it.)

"I'm turning in my license tomorrow morning. Mrs. St. Peter, nice to see you."

"I'm a very responsible driver, silly. I've seen *you* squeal out of the parking lot."

"I am visiting you for the first time in four months. Don't tell me about your driving privileges, tell me about your heart."

"Wait, what?"

"What you believe and whom you love and why the world will be better for having you in it. How's your mother?"

"In remission. The doctors are hopeful."

"Good. Do you still write poetry?"

"Sometimes."

"Good."

By the time the final horn sounded, the score was 41–7, and I felt wonderful. I had to round up Helen from the dark under the bleachers where she was talking to Marcus Tracey, a guidance counselor at MacKinley South whose integrity and heterosexuality I doubted, despite his wife and three children. I used to catch sight of Marcus on the drive to work every morning as he darted past me in excess of the speed limit, fiddling with his radio or cell phone or climate-control knobs. But he was an excellent counselor. If he planned Red Ribbon Week, you knew that the anti-drug slogans would be supported with reliable statistics and that the guest speaker he brought in would know how to make the girls cry with anecdotes about gray stillborn babies and lives lived in slavering alleys. I shook his hand with the special gusto I reserve for people I don't like.

"Marcus."

"Helen here's telling me about your new gig. Sounds sweet."

"Yeah, well." It always takes me a minute to warm back up to adult conversation, to find my way back into its ellipses and obfuscations. "It's not for the faint of heart."

"Counseling," he spat. "Fucking shit, it gets tiresome listening to kids talk about themselves all day. *Oh, mm hm, I'm totally fascinated to know who snubbed you at the dance, do you realize you smell like vinegar and have no interests?*" He was wearing a very nice blue oxford shirt, so nice I experienced it as an insult to me and all other men.

"Talk to you later, Marcus," Helen said, taking me by the wrist.

Only when we reached the crunching gravel of the lot, with the stadium glow behind us, did it occur to me that I had just cashed in fifteen years of camaraderie and good will for four quarters of football. To visit again would be pathetic, like the students we expel who hang around outside the gate at dismissal, leaning on their mud-flecked fenders and waiting for friends and girlfriends to emerge.

OUR FIRST day-long seminar was for the Mobile District Schools. We drove down the night before and wrestled around in the hotel room with *Little*

House on the Prairie playing. (Mary had broken her back, and Pa had to sell the farm and work in a mine to get money for the operation.) Helen rehearsed her introductory remarks, and we ordered a pizza with four kinds of meat. I don't like to rehearse. Any appeal I have as a speaker comes from the impression I give of spontaneous thought, of shooting from the hip and heart. Plus I was nervous, and I didn't want Helen to see that.

We mingled with the teachers over coffee and bagels from 8:30 to 9:00, and then we were on. Helen's opening went perfectly, exactly as it had in the hotel the night before. We were in a high school theater set up in the round for an upcoming production, and Helen made assured use of the teardrop stage, addressing the various compass points of the audience as if her scene had been blocked out in advance. She was wearing a red knee-length suit, and the shape of her calves was only enhanced by the bandage around her left ankle.

My function during her introduction was to look knowledgeable and click a few PowerPoint slides, but I felt the back of my neck grow cold as I watched her perform. She had her part *memorized*. I felt compromised by her excellence. These were the crucial moments, when the assembled teachers would decide just how much they hated us for despoiling a day of their lives, and Helen was going to pass them off to me attentive and optimistic, trusting against all precedent that I had something to offer that would enrich their careers. I reminded myself that lawyers, vice-principals, and politicians spoke every day in support of things they didn't really believe—I used to tell my classes that deceiving one another was how most of humanity made its living—but I still suffered a chill of horror when Helen said, "I'll turn the mike over now to Gerald Wellman, who's going to tell you a little more about what the switch to Standards-Based Education means." *You're up, hotshot,* she whispered as she made the hand-off.

My plan was to focus on a terrifically obese woman in the front row and let myself be guided, as I spoke, by sympathy for her daily trials. She looked heartsick and tired, with her twenty-year-old hairdo. How recently I would have been the one to whom she passed her listless notes! How recently I would have sat beside her making snide acronyms out of SBE to express my feeble outrage over our subjection to terminology and cant! I never wanted to return to that world again, that world of chalky impotence and makeshift collegiality, so I opened my mouth and spoke, and what emerged was a homily fueled not by sympathy, but by self-preservation:

"I am truly glad that you all have come here today. And I know why you came, you came because your principals forced you to"—a short pause for laughs, and then with all possible earnestness—"but also because you care about learning. You believe that learning is the purpose of life. You are the heads of Social Studies departments and English departments and Math departments, and you teach your students to value knowledge about the world around them. You are the heads of Science departments, that word that means knowledge. You know how to set high goals and inspire your students to crest or supersede them. You are the heads of Foreign Language. You go home at 6:00 with your eyes stinging, and you are tutoring again at 7:30 in the morning because you want what is best for the children in your care; you believe in some way having to do with human improvement and hope for the future that your life has meaning only to the extent that it serves the lives of others."

A short pause here, pregnant with sentiment, the speaker wrapped in private reflection.

"But what, you ask, does that belief have to do with Standards-Based Education, or SBE, as we'll be referring to it, and what does this man with ugly glasses and a Midwestern accent want from me? To which I say: nothing. Nothing that you don't want yourselves and that most of you don't already provide for your students. We will be presenting today an array of tools and techniques which may actually make your jobs easier while at the same time satisfying the State of Alabama. I'd like to begin, however, with a personality assessment activity, so if you'll kindly find the Peer Partner assigned to you on page seven of your binder. . . ."

I turned out to be, if not excellent, then at least moderately talented at consulting. Helen said as much more than once. She had preparation on her side—and marketing skills and a better command of recent educational research—but I projected the honesty and human directness that unified our message, that gave it a girth and fizzy essence. I flattered myself that I was the soul, as it were, in our steroidal body of lies.

So we clicked on graphs of student success and then stood in line at the bank to split our criminally large remittance. We visited Dollywood to sample the local handicrafts and then wowed the Sevier County Schools with a half day on Collaborative Learning. And then, sometime around Christmas, I realized I was in love with Helen. I saw her as a woman made wise and wary by a difficult marriage, and myself as the man who could wear away the shell of taciturnity which even her students remarked on and which I had tapped against experimentally in planes, in cars, and in the bed we shared, an ineffable, staunch sadness that colored all she did. I was attracted to her spartan lifestyle (generic shampoo, no cable), and to her oddball interests (collectible thimbles, the Electoral College). I admired her assertiveness behind the wheel of a car, the centrifugal on-ramp ascents. We were both over forty, and it was time to choose someone to cling to through the brittle-bone years, the drug-cocktail and tomato-garden years. But I'm making it sound as if I considered the issue before proceeding. I did not.

We were at the funeral of Harold Burgess on the 10th of December, a sunny day with icy, biting winds that seemed somehow more cruel because the sun was out. I watched Harold's easeled flowers get dismantled by the gusts as the pallbearers placed his husk at the frosty grave's lip—Harold, the grand old man of education in our town, forty-five years as a teacher, coach, and administrator, the kind of figure who could describe for students their parents' misdeeds in those selfsame classrooms, who spent whole periods in banter and reminiscence. At the end, in his twenty-second year at MacKinley South, he was back in the classroom, teaching European History to Honors seniors, many of whom were now huddled around the grave in twos and threes in inadequate winterwear. Even Helen, hungover and unable to check herself, was crying. Cash Monet found us in the crowd.

"He was just lecturing about Joan of Arc on Friday," Cash said, weeping lightly. "I think it was God's way of letting us know He was going to call Mr. Burgess home."

This is why I liked Cash Monet. He could talk intelligently about the reverence for the carnal in Whitman's poetry and also be capable of the most piercingly beautiful faith in God.

I meant something different than Cash would have, but I said, "We have to remember that he hasn't really died." Cash's face broke wide open as he nodded, and for a moment I was holding both Cash and Helen in my arms.

When Helen reached to start the car, I wrapped my hand over hers on the knurl of the ignition and said, "I love you. I want us to be together."

"What—oh, wow." She started crying again. She sat there in the deep seat of the new Acura we had bought and caught her grief, or whatever it was, in her left hand.

"Helen?"

She forced her breathing back to its normal pattern, pinching the bridge of her nose. The seat squeaked under her wool coat. The wind blew listing human figures across our windshield.

"I can't talk about this. Not today," and her hand twisted under mine as she started the car.

IT'S THE SECOND oldest story, I suppose. The oldest being desire, and the second—mine—being the confusion of desire with love. But I did love her. I succeeded in feeling for Helen the abandonment of self to the whimsical enterprise of another, and this abandonment didn't feel like a compromise, and it didn't rankle. I remember arguing with my ex-wife, Jean—I write her name here—over the way Tupperware should be stored in a cupboard and standing in front of the door where it went until she yielded. But with Helen my ego had been washed clean. Listening to her misstate my orders at drive-thru windows and shaving my beard on her request helped me achieve the sort of selflessness that some people spend years in the lotus position searching for. But ours was, finally, a contract born of selfishness, and try as I might to clothe and sweeten it, it returned soon enough to its original naked state.

Helen took me to dinner and told me she was letting me go, bringing Marcus Tracey on board. I'm still horrified by the inelegance of the scene—a Cajun restaurant with menus slicked by fingerprints, tipsy accordion from the jukebox, waitresses in shorts. The fact that the only thing visible in every direction from the asphalt parking lot was the landlocked terrain of central Alabama.

"The hell you are."

"We're going to make some changes and improvements."

"*I* want to make changes and improvements. That fairy?"

"We're going online."

"Why can't I do that?" I asked, afraid I was about to vomit étouffée. "I've been killing at these seminars."

"You haven't looked at the exit surveys, have you."

The wordless half-minute that followed, during which I thought of several fruitless protests I could make as someone abused cheap dishware in the kitchen, was mutually understood as my concession.

"This is awful of you, Helen. Truly awful."

"You made it awful. You made it that way."

She offered to drive me back to her place for my toothbrush and shampoo, my shaving kit. I declined. I wanted to think of my toiletries growing crusts of dust and germs on her vanity, infecting and ravaging her the way she had infected and ravaged me.

AND SO—if I leave out six weeks of moping and the schemes of sabotage and defamation I considered and a couple of reprehensible late-night phone calls to Jean, who is remarried—that's how I ended up at Johnson County High School, teaching three sections of AP English and two sections of Expository Writing. This is a big building, with a couple thousand students whose names I'll never know, and I like it that way. I pee next to teachers with strange faces and blank pasts. The male students, who are allowed to wear baseball caps inside the building, all look the same to me, and the girls look either angry or frightened. Perhaps I exaggerate. A few students in my AP classes show flashes of courage, but they've propped it up with an idealism that is equal parts computer animation and Bible School. On Monday, Teresa Pohlmann, fixing her jet-black ponytail, told me I was wrong to call the fly in Dickinson's poem an image of despair and obliteration; it was, instead, an emblem of nature's caring touch in our final moment. God sends the fly to usher the dying soul to heaven, something like that. For once, it didn't seem my place to challenge such tender folly. Teresa Pohlmann will believe in death soon enough.

Then there are the disillusioned, like Steven Casper. Steven slouches and doodles his way through third period, sketching dicks and fighter planes in the margins of his notebook. (There are no notes.) I call his mother, and she seems preoccupied by something, maybe Judge Judy or Judge Mathis. As far as I can discover, the worst blow Steven has suffered is that he's realized he won't be as rich as TV has promised him. But who knows? Maybe he grew up under a tree in the woods where kids make their own houses and are their own parents; maybe he's learned that everyone is selling something all the time. I took him to the McDonald's across the street to discuss his academic progress, and we ended up having an hour-long conversation about Viking ship construction as the kids in Playland beaned each other with plastic balls. How the lumber was cured, how the sails were sewn, how navigation was accomplished. I ate my deadly fries and listened to Steven. As children yelled and ducked outside the glass, I imagined our hairy forebears in the prows of those proud vessels, those crafts of timber and hubris, daring the ocean swell in search of something they had never seen before.

How I Come to Be Here at the GasFast

WELL, OFFICER, I'm watching Michael Jackson and Kofi Annan on TV. Yes, that's true, it is my second night here.

You wouldn't say this was my so-call cosmic plan.

What happened would be it started with I purchase a scratch ticket and I'm scratching it in my truck, out by the pump. On the steering wheel, pressing light so you don't accidental honk. So I scratch five dollars and proceed the ticket inside to redeem my winnings.

So, OK. My truck and my implements is all filled up. The engine is running as I'm scratching is how close I am to leaving. But I idle forward into the location you see it, the double-axle Ford there with the trailer. Appreciate it. I wash it every Monday and maintenance all the et cetera. It's my pride possession. You're right about that, it does go through some gas.

Right, so I get my five tickets and transgress them over here by the TVs to this seating area to perform my scratching, and lo behold, I win fifty dollars. The radio has prewarn me there's a accident on St. Claude, which is my artery home. So I say, you might as well enjoy a snack and relax at the provided tables. Which they wouldn't have these tables they didn't want you to use them. Driver's license? Here you go. Last ticket 1979, thirty-two in a poorly mark school zone. I believe in you follow the laws, including speeding. I'm of the opinion what's the hurry. Everybody love where they're going that much?

Right, yes sir, so they had *Jeopardy* going on one TV and *Jerry Springer* on the other, and my snack at the time consist of convenient-sized Doritos, if you're noting this down, and the subject was, what was it, it was, "Help, My Mom Is a Whore."

No, no family. Had a wife, which this would now be ten years ago, who there were irreconcilable differences with my career vocation. Meaning if I said, That would be interesting, being a chef, or, That would be interesting, being a specialize mechanic on German cars, she would research the topic and bug me constant about do that, stop mowing lawns. They had a thing where you apply for a class and they take you through the engine. She had a mental picture of I'm professional attired doing computer diagnose on BMWs, so on and so for. Hm? Just up the road, right across the Parish line. I got half a shotgun double. Yep, I got a dog, but the neighbor feeds him too.

Well, how I been solving that is they have a trucker shower round back. Six dollars, all tile, very nice, and the pressure's better than at home.

You think you know what's in a convenience store, but you don't. You are aware they have whatever brand of cigarettes, and you can locate your accustom beer, but here's a question: do they have garden gloves? Yes, they do. Do they have a coloring book of, like, extinct birds? Yes, they do. Do they have this T-shirt I am wearing which on the inside-out has Britney Spears? And you are looking at the answer. Your question, do they have food you can exist indefinitely, and since you're writing this down, the answer is last night I purchased a national-brand frozen dinner and cooked it in the provided microwave, chicken marwhatever and baby peas, I would give it seven out of ten, and tonight you see I am leisurely enjoying a bag of Sun Crisps follow by two turkey-meat hot dogs from the deli amenity, which they wouldn't inform you the fat content on a poster if they didn't want you to sit and enjoy, along with this personal-size bottle of blush wine, followed by afterwards this individual-wrap oatmeal cookie. And after Michael's face melt off, which I predict at most another five minutes, I have this toothbrush I selected from the hygiene little section to service myself dentally. Do they have travel-size pretty much everything you would ever need for your mouth? Yes, they do.

Why should they care, as long as I am continuous purchasing?

I would like to state for the record that as a black man, I have inquiries about both these individuals. Michael Jackson, it's like you're watching one of those movies with an unknown microbiology, the moon comes out and he turns into a thousand spiders. Figure out its details, and you can overconquer it, does it lay eggs, does it travel by sewer. Is there an existing spray. On the other hand of the coin, you have Kofi. A man who whenever he opens his mouth, everybody claps. He is accompany by constant clapping. Stand up they clap, sit down they clap. Tell them what you ate for breakfast, they clap. He leaves work, and people are standing in the door clapping.

Do I have lawns to mow? That's the question I been asking myself. I have if you look at my trailer I've got two push mowers, three trimmers, two leaf blowers, and four proper receptacles for fuel, which it takes I would calculate fifteen minutes to fill these items. Let's say this occurs three times in your given week. OK, so this morning I am sitting here looking out at my implements and the sun is rising and I am asking your exact question. But I'm also thinking how every piece of equipment is topped off to the top, and why should I start expending them? Because if I expend them, where will I be? Back here paralleling up to the pump and going through the procedure. You have days where all you think about is gas. You have a picture in your mind of how much this tool has and how much that tool has, you're standing inside the tank in your mind and the gas is up to here or here. I have gas constant on my mind, and I have onkeeping schemes of when I stop one tool and start another tool, et cetera. I have dreams at night of if the gas runs out, I die. So I am sitting here this morning, and the sun is coming up to grow back all the grass I cut yesterday, and the question is what am I getting done going in these circles? When the sun is working against me?

Last night? I will tell you for your written record. I ate my frozen dinner, and I was watching the Hornets game, and I would say halftime was the last moment I had thoughts of maybe I should leave. Mid-season NBA, you're thinking what does this game mean, which the answer is nothing, and I'm watching drug dealers roll up to the pumps with luxury rims. Chief over there, who I'm presuming called you regarding me, has start giving me looks, plus these benches aren't designed for long-term comfort where a person's buttocks are concern. So, OK, but the first play of the second half is a dunk by Tyson Chandler, one of those where his arm seems to longate from ten feet away, and it occurs to me this is a indication game. Of can we beat the Dallases and the San Antonios. Can we beat the Atlantas. So I get interested on that basis. I'm walking around during a timeout, and over by the Styrofoam coolers I find this seat cushion. Which it says Hornets on it. Which I buy utilizing my winnings. Which then there is post-game and the late news, all the David Letterman shows. And I purchase a soft-serve cone from the ice cream area.

Wait now: I'll read off the TV and you guess which: *This is an issue not for any one state, but for the international community as a whole.* That's correct, Kofi. *States and people around the world attach fundamental importance to such legitimacy, and to the international rule of law.* Why you're not clapping, officer? Everyone has to obligatory clap. Pardon? Am I here as a war protest? No, sir, I got a nephew in Iraq.

I would like to add this to the discussion since you're noting this: where is all their grass? If we export some grass, maybe they won't be so disgruntle.

Well, you know, I don't get tired here. It's the lights maybe. There is also the refill coffee, which I have liberally partook. But it's also I'm taking a interest in the world. I'm standing still and everyone else is moving and I am watching. This equates to I am learning. I read the paper, including I consider the editorials and work the Jumble. I have seen two friends from many years past, one of who being Monkey Bones, I can't remember his real name, out of prison and now he's janitorial at Murphy Oil, and then in walks Myron Metcalf in a suit and tie. This is a kid who used to set things on fire in the neighborhood, and now he's the publications are under his supervise at the art museum. We called him Fyron. I'm even watching the commercials with I guess you could call it a sense of wow. This napkin here's a tally of how many males in commercials versus females, one hour, both TVs. Up to when you walked in, it's 171 to 171, plus two I couldn't tell. That's luminating. I have also notice people are wearing yellow in many commercials. Many people are getting sprayed with liquid. They showed a show on Palestine, where it came from. They showed a show on bees. So the thing of sleeping is, what will you miss? Because there is infinite amounts to know and understand.

OK, guess: *I'm thinking about adopting two kids from each continent around the world, that is my dream.* Correct, Michael. White babies, black babies, chink babies. We are the world, naked in his swimming pool.

Right, so I won the thousand at three-thirty this afternoon. This would be Wednesday, Central Time, if you're writing this down. After dinner and a ice cream cone and a toothbrush and a shower and a seat cushion, my fifty-dollar winnings were nearly deplete, so I spent the last seven dollars on tickets, and lo behold, the first one I scratch, I win. Which they don't redeem that kind of sum direct, so chief there agreed to buy it from me on a personal basis for nine hundred. Which I think you should be asking who can call their girlfriend and five minutes later she is showing up with nine hundred dollars cash in her sock? Point is, my opinion, they got real crimes being committed around us. They got murders and theft. They got gas prices are going up despite my nephew is standing in front of a oil rig with a M-16.

But, OK, I will leave. But you should write I have stated I could continue. You should write I have become conscious of my job does not make sense as a human. We take the gas out of the ground and use it back on the ground, which to me, our brains are better than this. To me, we have curiosity for knowledge which isn't being satisfy. After you, officer. I would like to know more about the quote Holy Land, who has possession. I would like to know about what have you on the Discovery Channel, volcanoes and coral. You maybe don't think about it because you're young, but you will reach a age. It will strike you where are all these people hurrying so fast? What is that smell in the air? Why does there always have to be a smell?

SAINTS AND MARTYRS

I WOKE TO a trailer of costumes on my lawn and the smell of Don Violet in my house.

Don was still using Speed Stick then, the cinnamon kind, and his morning smell made me think of medieval times, cuts of meat preserved with holiday spices. A cook with dirty hands slices off the next gray hunk; outside the castle walls, lots of hay and plague. Who knows where the brain gets its junk, but the next stop for mine was usually 1977, tenth grade, when so many boys were wearing cinnamon Speed Stick that I thought it was the natural smell of making out in a car, of boys themselves, of the whole unexplored body of the future. Then the future exposes itself with its daily flasher's trick, and all its smells go stale. I saw no reason to hurry out of bed.

If the Ursuline nuns had told me at sixteen that I would someday gauge the location of a boyfriend by reference to cured flesh, I might have considered the vocations they were always making us pray for at Mass. But the nuns didn't know much about flesh, and I'm not sixteen, I'm forty-six, and I have characteristic smells of my own. The thing about being sixteen is that you're eager to devote your life to ideas. The thing about being forty-six is that you've traded most of your ideas for practical wisdom: How to judge the viciousness of a hangover from the pull on the string between your eyes. (I'd had worse.) How to run a systems check for any body parts you may have mistreated. (My right ankle felt a little swollen.)

How to lie perfectly still as your memory stalks back so that if it has sharp teeth, it's less likely to pounce and maul you.

My heart stumbled on its runway, my stomach squirled. My face resolved into a dew. How long I lay suffering the special torment of the self, I couldn't say, because even though the sun sneaked up my arm and a church bell kept wangling the half hours, there was no such thing as time anymore. This was the October right after the storm, three weeks after they'd let us back into the city, and the clocks were still broken. I don't know how else to put it. Time had gone offline with the traffic lights and the mayor's brain, and there were no signs it was coming back. It was hiding in a hotel in Houston maybe, watching four hours of CNN and stepping outside for a smoke. Or it was holed up in the Irish Channel with a handgun, not trusting the all-clear. The water had stopped just short of my house, but the limbo had found us all, and I was in a kind of desperate love with it, I yearned to disappear inside it and add my waste to the flotsam of the city, both of us someone's former dream left in dashed and soggy piles. OK, fine, but when was someone going to come pick up the trash?

Later, in the front room, my memory of the trailer on the lawn and the trailer itself collided as I edged the curtain for a look outside, the two meeting in reality with an unassailable thump. There it was, the inscrutable cube of it, as if deposited by science fiction. I flipped a card or two in my brain, hoping to pair the trailer with something known, but the deck was too big and blind to yield any hits, so I gave up and went to the kitchen.

That's where I found Don, balled up in front of my new fridge, shirtless and plaintive on the tile. I rounded him and eased the door, which cleared his ear neatly and hung its jars of olives and relish over his head. A ring of gold around his mouth revealed that he had been provisioning himself from his collapse, and I finally matched the color to a bag of butterscotch chips. Where Don had gotten the unfamiliar black trousers he was wearing, shiny and way too small and dotted with lint, was a question much less pressing than what I had come for: ice in a glass, coffee trickled in, jot of milk, straw from the cupboard. Gingerly to the breakfast bar, from which angle Don wasn't the most attractive sight, with the bottoms of his feet gone gray and his ass flattened into the trousers, but I spent most of the next half hour with my eyes closed anyway. Plus, as long as Don Violet was drooling on his cheek and whimpering, *Mom, I'm cold,* self-reproach would have no business to conduct with me.

Finally I stood over him and willed him to consciousness.

"Mom?"

"No, it's Janet."

"Help me."

There followed some heaving and ho-ing on my part, some squinting and brittle kneeling on his, followed by a fruitless search for his shirt. Then I took him outside for a look at the trailer. I have a typical New Orleans front yard, which means that even though the trailer was at most ten feet long, it blocked both my porch steps and the sidewalk. The riddle of how we had backed the trailer between my duct-taped fridge at the curb and my neighbor's, exactly what mischief we'd made of the night, could have possibly been deciphered from the pictogram of muddy tracks in the grass, but Don, struck by the sudden sunlight, wrung his eyes like a vampire and fell back against the cool aluminum flank of the trailer, concentrating against a sudden gush of sweat.

"Shady side feels good," he remarked, as if we were thinking of keeping it. The lettering above his head said *Fradella's Film and Stage Rentals*. For all my life, until I saw Don pressed against that trailer, I had been deprived of a full understanding of the word *clammy*, but Don remedied that omission with his lucent seafoam pallor, his six wilted chest hairs, the cold tumble of his love handles over the waistband of those alien pants.

"Wait, do you even have a hitch on your car?" he asked.

"I do."

"No shit."

The line of fridges up and down the block breathed its funk into the street like a row of bad teeth. But even the smell couldn't mask the fact that it was a gorgeous day. I know a lot of people who moved to New Orleans after first seeing it in October or November, and here was the beauty they'd been powerless against: the elysian green of trees rustling against themselves with pleasure, the inside of things at peace with the outside, the air so soft it promises that suffering doesn't have to be constant.

"I'm just going to rest here for a moment," Don said, lifting his closed eyes to the breeze and letting his body slide down the side of the trailer. I went inside to shower.

WHO WAS Don Violet to me? He was the boy down the block who vomited at my fifth birthday party with a paper cone sliding off his head, signaling that he was in some way specially mine, just as I signaled that I was his by breaking my arm in his driveway a month later. He was the seventh grader who looked up with watery eyes from Tarzan novels to read my notes about how Carmen Pellegrini was a total slut. He was the person to whom I first showed mine and who first showed me his, a man who seemed destined to live with his mother until she died and perhaps beyond, as in the stories. He was a recreational alcoholic with truly egregious teeth and an acid tongue that hid the fact that there were actually things he believed in. He could not, even a little bit, drive a stick-shift; he was physically incapable of running; he was a collector of very strange art and the chair of a high school English department. He was the man I could not break free of, just as I was the woman he could not break free of, one of the great givens of my life, like Catholicism and orange hair.

We dialed the number on the trailer. Don had gone back to his house to recover his dignity and returned with fried seafood in Styrofoam.

"We've got your stuff," I said to the kid who answered.

"OK."

"The film rentals or whatever?" I watched Don's eyes cross to the oyster in his fingers. "Is what it says on the trailer?"

"Oh, right on, the costumes. We totally needed those today."

He's high, I mouthed.

"You kept Jude Law waiting. People were super-pissed."

This dropping of an actor's name brought me to a point of terminal boredom, like the Emmys, Grammys, and Oscars.

"That does sound tragic. You want it back?"

"Yeah, just I guess drop it back in the lot. Where you got it from." The word *lot* strung behind it a few of the details I'd so far been unable to resurrect: Don and I giggling across Esplanade Avenue toward the weedy acre where St. Aloysius High School used to be, now an empty urban scrub parked with film trucks and yellowed by street lights; Don's orange polo shirt, too small and making his head look enormous as we skulked around; the two of us scrambling into the cab of an unlocked semi and counting the amphetamines in the glove box. None of which quite solved the mystery of the trailer on my lawn, any more than just taking it back would provide a satisfying climax to whatever diversion Don and I had been trying to script for ourselves.

"I'm going to need a finder's fee. Some consideration for returning it."

Don's eyebrows became interested.

"I'm confused," the boy stated with touching honesty. "You didn't find it, you stole it."

"I didn't say I did. Let's say I didn't. Let's say I found it, and what's it worth to have it back."

"OK, why would I not call the police?"

"I'm a lawyer. I know all those guys."

"That doesn't sound right. My mom's a lawyer."

"Your attitude is very off-putting. I'm going to call back in five minutes, and we'll see if you've changed your tune."

I set the cordless on the bar.

"Smooth," Don said.

"What the fuck. Hollywood thinks it's going to show up *now* and not get looted?"

"It's not Hollywood. It's a local rental company supplying Hollywood."

"Westbank. You call that local?"

Don and I were of the same mind about the Westbank, just as we were about the Northshore, Kenner, and most of the suburbs: it was crass, ugly, and awful, populated by people who poached their wages from the city and fled to enroll their daughters in strip-mall dance schools, people who honeymooned in Disney and named their kids *Chase* and *Madison,* who spoke of themselves as living in New Orleans but whose values were as alien to the city as if they lived in Nebraska. It was the Westbank sheriff, Arthur Lawson, who earned the gratitude of his constituents after the storm by firing over the heads of the mostly black Orleanians who tried to cross the Mississippi bridge in search of food and water.

"Under normal circumstances, no. But under the circumstances of we've got a stolen trailer on the lawn that we're adding what would it be, extortion to, I think it's probably time to get rid of it."

"Who's Jude Law again?"

"Same person as Claire Danes, I think."

We devoted ourselves to curative grease. The shrimp and oysters came from a Spur station, one of the few places open, and anyway where I had always gotten the second-best po-boy in the city. With each bite, a little more of my misery softened and sighed away.

"Do you have grading to do?" I asked.

"Yes, but no. I'll do it in the morning." That was the semester Don's school day started at 4:00 P.M.; his campus had gone under seven feet of water, and they were holding classes at night, in another school's building. "I need a sharp mind to properly appreciate the argument that if guns are outlawed, then only outlaws will have guns."

Don forms sentences with the slight retard you expect from an English teacher, his mind running five or six words ahead to select vocabulary and round the syntax. He pretends to be exasperated by his students, but what really exasperates him is their parents—the spoiling and kowtowing, the catering to needs that don't exist until the parents create them, the bequeathing of acquisitiveness and self-satisfaction. "Because first off is outlaws don't respect the law. This is proven by many of statistics."

"Like as in you're 80% full of shit, son."

"But Mr. Violet, I gave 110% on this paper."

"Divided by you're illiterate."

We might have gone on like this until we sighed with overfed stupor and stumbled off for a nap if the phone, which lay between us on the bar, had not started ringing.

"Yello."

"Just letting you know I called the police."

"Whoa, jeez. I'm bringing your stupid trailer back."

"Too late. Call's made."

"On who? You don't know who I am."

"Sure I do. Ever hear of caller I.D. and the Internet?"

"That's not sporting."

"If you still live at 7726 Plum, I recommend you get ready to answer the door."

Don looked carefully at the phone where I set it.

"I don't mean to alarm you," I said, "but."

He squeaked his food closed and grabbed paper towels for the road.

"HOLY JESUS!" I yelled a minute later, jabbing the volume down, "did we really have the radio on that loud?"

"You were singing along with 'Ride of the Valkyries.'"

"I don't know the words to that shit."

"Nevertheless."

"Does it even have words? I mean—"

A trio of police cars screamed into my mirror. There was one in each lane of the three-lane road we were on, a squadron sweeping upon us in urban majesty. I released the chemicals of remorse and amnesia into my bloodstream as I navigated toward the shoulder, my knees going foggy— but before I could come to a stop, the cruisers swept past us in flotilla, their sirens' pitch shrugging with lost interest.

"Such an iconic American moment," Don said appreciatively. "Cops in the rearview mirror."

"Fuck America," I said, jarred out of my wits.

My mother lived in the part of Old Metairie where elderly people who spoke eloquently about the past glories of the city lived. In keeping with her surroundings, she employed vintage terminology for black people, gay people, Asians, Muslims—or, if forced to, used newer terms as if handling a dirty rag, held far away and released with a sniff. For truly exceptionable topics, she'd retained a dozen of the Italian expletives my grandparents had brought from Sicily. Sitting as she did atop the ridge in Old Metairie that hadn't flooded, flanked now by empty waste, she seemed more than ever a resolute totem who'd climbed to a perch to let time flow beneath her, watching four daily local newscasts, working EZ crossword puzzles, and freezing family-sized batches of food.

"You want me to be an accessory to theft."

"Mom, I didn't say theft." But since my mother *couldn't hear,* as she put it, *foolishness and nonsense,* she continued to sight me up over the half-glasses she used for puzzles, pointing at her incapacitated ears. I had been compulsively tracing one of the eggplants printed on her vinyl table-cloth, and now I found myself ridiculously unable to lift my finger, as if it was the only thing holding down the cursive caption: *Eggplant.* "I just want to roll it behind your house and get it later. You need to move your car for just like two seconds."

"Donald," she said, using the form of his name she'd used when, at seven, he had broken her porcelain statue of Mary and tried to hide the shards, "come outside with me."

As Don played stagehand to the huge production that was my mother firing up and undocking her Lincoln Continental, I got behind the wheel of my own car to face the mortal terror of backing a trailer through a narrow space. Ninety-nine percent of human history had no knowledge of this fear, and I luxuriated in self-pity for all the ways I was beset by modernity as I waited for Don and my mom. Don came strolling across the lawn with an impish grin that said something in the world had turned out exactly as he'd expected it to, and I knew my mother had treated him to a sampler of her choicest phrases. Don's snaggled teeth, leaping in front of each other like vaudeville rivals, helped me see the humor in what Mom did next: backing the Lincoln not into the street but in a nutty arc across the lawn, she surged forward and barricaded her driveway against me, one wheel lodged in each of the azalea beds she had planted decades earlier in some flowering of hope. As a symbolic act, it was beyond improvement.

"I love her," Don said as she stared at us through her passenger window, a glassy gray icon.

For me, the glories of the city are not in the past, and weren't even that October. For industry, maybe. For artists and loafers looking to duck the firefight of the economy, probably. For the age-old meaning of our neighborhoods, definitely and tragically. But that vital, indefinable something was still in the air as Don and I transported our pillage, that deep breathing of the city that reminded you everyplace else was dead. Now, three years later, when the real hangover has set in, it's difficult to recapture the thrill and relief of returning to New Orleans; but on the night of the costumes, Don and I were still feeling the flush we'd felt the morning we waited at the Parish line for the National Guard to open our zip code, and we'd spent the lost and endless month of September in a collection of noplaces: the hotel in Vicksburg where we evacuated with our mothers; the motel in a dry county in Arkansas, wherever that is; after that, a few days for me in Alexandria and for Don in Hammond; and finally, the starkest of horrors, a two-week purgatory in that least human of all human places, Baton Rouge; and although the city we found inside the checkpoint was a soundless waste dipped in death and muck, New Orleans was the most beautiful place either one of us had ever seen.

So when we'd come out of the bar and started poking around those trucks and trailers, it was in part with the wonder of returning to a life of three dimensions.

"Port of Call," I said, naming the bar with a finger snap.

"Correct. I had a burger. And two lukewarm pickles."

"Our waiter had a soul patch thingy."

"And a degree in English but no knowledge of the subjunctive. *If I was you, I'd try the pork chop.*"

My car found the corners out of Mom's neighborhood, and I could feel the rest of last night, all its details, waiting just around the next few corners of my mind if I would only let my thoughts choose their course, the way the details of a dream linger outside memory until they invite themselves in on the smell of laundry or a laugh on the radio. But my dreams tend to feature implacable spiders or, far too often, female body builders—not unlike my actual nights of drinking—so I held those monsters at bay by snatching up my phone and dialing the known monster of the present, boy Fradella.

"OK, that was rude. Didn't I say I was bringing it back?"

"After I called the cops. Aren't lawyers supposed to be good at before and after?"

"Psh," I spat. "I'm not *that* kind of lawyer."

"OK," he said, talking to someone in the room. "My dad says to tell you we spent six hundred bucks on replacement stuff so we could shoot. If you want to reimburse that, we'll call off the dogs."

"You must be joking."

"If I was joking, you'd be laughing."

"You weren't this precocious two hours ago."

"I don't really wake up till like six at night."

I closed the phone and handed it to Don. You could tell he'd never owned a cell phone from the too careful way he held it, as if cradling a gerbil.

"What time is it?" I asked.

Don wears his watch loose and has to double-twist his wrist to read it. "Going on 5:30."

"Want to just unhitch this thing at Winn-Dixie?"

Don shrugged and made a noncommittal bleat high in his throat, as if to suggest he wasn't necessarily ready to cut it loose yet, that the scenario hadn't carried us as deeply or richly through our Sunday as it had promised.

"We're only a few blocks from my house," he proposed. "Let's drink about ten gallons of water and then see how we feel."

Don's father, before he died ten years ago, was a neurosurgeon, and the house he left his family is a neurosurgeon's house, three stories of salmon-colored stucco, arched windows, a palatial terra-cotta roof. The oak-lined street it sits on is so tucked away from the normal economy of Uptown streets that we probably could have left the trailer there for months without it ever being noticed.

I suppose every woman who lives to eighty becomes a character of some sort. My mother was the sort of character who drank exactly seven beers a week and believed that all the Saints' problems would be solved if they had a white quarterback. Don's mother, Marion, is the sort of character who calls the Pope *Holy Father* and studies local Catholic programming. Women our mothers' age sit at kitchen tables, not on couches, and that's where we found Don's mother, in a kitchen chair accomplishing one more of the afternoons before death.

"Hi, Donnie. What's in your trailer?"

She had seen our approach right through the walls with her Jesus-vision.

"School stuff."

I kissed her powdery cheek.

"Hello, Janet, sweetie."

Marion looked upon me much as my mother looked upon Don, as the representation of a colossal failure, but one she couldn't hold against me with full stridency because I had once been a child in her house. She looked younger than my mother, her hair a jet-puffed mahogany, because she had the money to bring functionaries to bear on her body, just as she always seemed to have several Mexican youths addressing the bushes in her front yard. She was as agreeable as a person who told you she prayed for you and who based all her votes on one issue could be.

"There's some prosciutto I got today."

Don was digging around in the fridge.

"What's this in the cellophane?"

"Mushrooms with crab meat."

This was Marion's miracle: food occurred in her wake, lasagnas and stuffed artichokes manifesting under her fingertips in quantities that would have made sense only if Don's father or any of his five siblings had still been in the house. Don grabbed the mushrooms, a stem of grapes, and four stalks of celery. We genuflected before the matriarch and went upstairs to Don's room.

I could never enter Don's room without a pinch of nostalgia for the way I first knew it, as a jumblescape of Legos and Hot Wheels and science sets and cap guns where the constant peril of stepping on something sharp was balanced by the excitement of stumbling upon a toy you hadn't seen before. I remember dressing up his G.I. Joes, the old-fashioned ones with whiskered hair and gun-grip hands, their shirts that fastened with tiny metal snaps. I remember poking around in the attic and finding a box of his parents' albums, Frank Sinatra, Jo Stafford, Louis Prima, and playing them on a suitcase turntable with gold buckles, unaware in a way ten-year-olds can't possibly be anymore that the music wasn't current. I remember the time we tried on each other's clothes in the closet. My parents moved six times when I was growing up; so, far from having a warm enclosure of my own whose shapes matched the shapes of my consciousness, I had a series of rooms that I knew the way college students know apartments, skimming them just long enough to pass the test and move on. So while my financially ill-favored father rousted us from house to house and himself into an early grave, I packed my Barbies in a tote and took them over to Don's. I've more or less kept some of my things there ever since. From 1990 to '92, when Don was engaged to Paulette Theriot, I didn't visit much. And then there was that unfortunate episode in '03 when I tried to seduce the senior partner of my firm after his wife died—he was seventy-seven, but I'd caught him looking at my ass—and Don, ferreting out my plot, called me a *dirty whore,* and I didn't talk to him for a year. But even then he didn't throw out my toothbrush and T-shirts. So maybe we were propped against a different headboard and watching *Jeopardy* instead of *The Electric Company,* and instead of Spiderman posters, Don's walls were hung with several examples of the truly screwy art he now prefers, but it was still the place where we had derived our own natural laws and could live within their protections.

"Have I told you how much I loathe this motherfucker?" one of us said.

We were referring to the robot champion who had swept away all sense of proportion on *Jeopardy* with his hypocritical smugness and weenie's voice and the unfamiliar tenets of his faraway faith.

"Mormon bastard's just going to throw ten percent of it into the maw of the church."

"He'll be quite a catch for some young lady and her four sisters. Wait," I said, "did we—do you remember wearing muumuus?"

"I do," Don answered in a way that suggested that if I insisted on pressing forward, he could not be blamed for what I might find there.

"Yeah. We pulled over in the Robért's at Elysian Fields? We got the flashlight and went inside the trailer? I tried to put on that lollipop-kid outfit with the red suspenders, but the shorts got stuck halfway up my legs? And you came out of the trailer in that purple muumuu."

That looks damn comfortable, I'd remarked in the dark echo of the parking lot, which is how we ended up at Markey's Bar in the Bywater in matching muumuus, our bodies enjoying their own naked shapes beneath thin drapery. Don argued with the guy next to him about Deuce MacAlister and the I-formation, tracing running routes on the bar with an arm whose biceps was trimmed in a white ruffle.

"Do you know how loose and free I was?" I asked.

"I had a breeze whisking directly across my jim-jam."

Final Jeopardy was STATE CAPITALS, and something about the terrible blandness of the clue (Easternmost capital) and the dry anticlimax of the answer (Dover) made me want to fuck. It was as if I could feel the clue lifting from the screen and brushing over my skin in all its studious rectitude, and my skin responded by flashing open with need. I wanted to press myself against something and be pressed, I wanted to be bustled about on a soft surface, to be out of breath in that very particular way. I always get horny when I have a hangover, so it didn't surprise Don when I pulled his hand between my legs, putting some force behind it to let him know he didn't need to waste time. He unzipped me and sighted his target, and I pulled off his shirt and T-shirt because I think it's weird when a fully clothed man goes down on you. There's no way to hide the fact that neither of us is much to look at. Don is slim, but he's maintained his slimness by slowly ceding his muscles, so that his visual effect is soft and milky, like boiled veal. He has highly vivid and embarrassing nipples. For my part, I'm too small for comment on top and too big to avoid it on bottom, my great round hillock of an ass making me look ridiculous in all clothes and more ridiculous out of them. I am, from the waist down, absolutely impervious to all diets and forms of exercise. It's my huge ass that is, in some way, the source of all my humiliations and overachievements, the way the Civil War is for the South. And then there's my abhorrent skin: like many red-headed women, my skin was celestially perfect until I was eleven, at which point it turned into the blotchy detriment I own today.

But we're nice to touch. Don feels ambrosial in your hands, mallowy and yielding, like icing in a bag. And Don says he loves my ass, and I know he's telling the truth from the way he gathers it up when he does his silent work, his arms under and around me as if carrying a double load of treasure.

When Marion knocked, Don looked up petulantly from his task, and I grabbed his ear to make sure he didn't get away.

"Donnie? Janet?" (The door was locked.)

"Yes, Mother."

"I'm putting in garlic bread for dinner. Do you want garlic bread?"

"Yes, please," Don lilted, his smile setting again beneath the curve of my belly.

I think about the way things move forward and backward. My mom did nothing to control her diabetes, either before or after the storm, and I knew she probably wouldn't live another five years, and that, even if she did, she wouldn't really be alive for them anyway, all her best energies spent replaying the scenes in her memory. Don's mom still interacted with people in the world, arguably improving it with her charitable soups and raffles, but her real life lay even further back than my mom's, with Father Seelos and Mother Cabrini and all the saints and martyrs who have done the Church's will throughout the ages. If this was a sickness, then maybe it was the sickness of our city, which dreamed backward with all the best parts of itself, squinting against the harsh light of the present, and would return to primeval swamp if it had its way. And it was my sickness too. I stayed current on real estate law and put money in my 401K and read the A-section of the *Times-Picayune,* but none of these things had reality for me. For me, the real world was still a place where you sneaked upstairs to misbehave, where everything you could touch was a toy.

Because it was the déjà vu of that moment, Don's interrupted head rising from between my legs, that brought the two fronts of my memory, the forward and the backward, crashing together. I knew where Don's missing shirt was and what those black trousers were. The full flood of memory rose up around me as Don's efforts circled home to their goal.

"Oof," I shivered as he knee-walked up the bed. "That definitely works better without an audience."

"Ronnie Guidry," he said, timbering to his pillow.

Don's missing shirt was in the back of my SUV, exactly where I had wadded and thrown it right before a flashlight had shoved its wide eye up against the rear window. Drunk as I was, I thought Don had lit a flare or something between my legs, and I kicked his head away, the recoil sending my feet so far over my shoulders I wasn't sure I'd be able to right myself again. Don worked his bare arms into a tuxedo jacket and popped the hatch, and I crawled out behind him through a hiss of crinoline to find myself pantiless in a wedding dress amidst the humid live oaks of City Park, squinting at a cop.

After a brief once-over, he doused the flashlight. The moonlight showed him to be barely more than a kid, yellow hair glassed with product and cheeks innocent of a razor.

"Y'all . . . just married?"

"Yep," I confirmed with lawyerly facility. It sounded nicer than admitting we had raided the clothes from the trailer in hopes of scoring free omelets at the Clover Grill.

The kid was obviously no Sherlock Holmes: Neither Don nor I was wearing a ring, our clothes fit like After attire on Before people, and we were standing in front of a trailer with the words *Film Rentals* blazoned in red letters. Then Don was apparently blowing our cover.

"Wait a second, is that Ronnie Guidry?"

"Yes, sir," the kid answered tentatively.

"You colored your hair."

"Mr. Violet?"

"Ronnie Guidry! You SOB!"

They slapped each other's backs, their words and bodies relaxing into the joy of the hallways and classrooms where they had known each other. This happened everywhere we went, Don's former students crowding our table in restaurants or yelling us down in the parking garage at Saints games. My role was to stand aside and marvel not only that Don always remembered their names—they all looked the same to me—but that he also remembered where they had gone to college and how many siblings they had and what their parents did. Add the kids Don has taught to the people he knows from thirty years of being in a krewe and to the doctors and lawyers he knows through his father and me, and you can see why Don is one of the people who make New Orleans a place where six degrees of separation is way more than you need to get the job done, like using a slide rule for addition.

"Your mom and them's OK?"

"They're over in Birmingham in a hotel." He couldn't seem to decide whether this was a sign of civilization or apocalypse. "House is trashed."

"The school had about seven feet."

"Yeah, I drove past."

No wonder our clown show didn't register for Ronnie Guidry: his vision was full, overtopped by the things he'd seen in the last two months, the ruined school and house, the starved pets and stray bullets, bodies probably, whatever else a cop who stayed through the storm saw, and his eyes had no room left for the streaming present.

"How are you?" Don asked in that teacher's voice that allows no evasions. "You OK?"

"Oh, yeah," Ronnie said, waving lightly. "I'm fine."

Hearing what he'd said, Ronnie Guidry laughed twice, *ha ha,* as if experimentally. Then his laugh kicked up, the way it does when the absurd has come too close and you need to push it away. Don had a long acquaintance with the absurd and returned a laugh of his own, and this encouraged a less contained kind of laughter from Ronnie Guidry; and then Don was yodeling up to his loony giggle, which always reminds me of a goat, and this brought my own cackling out among the echoes we were making across the dead and soundless park. Ronnie's polite lie was funny because it was so fantastic and because it was the same fantastic lie all of us had told ourselves by coming back and continuing to believe that the life we had known was still here: the changeless green-shouldered levees where people jogged and walked their dogs; the drumlines and air horns of prep football; the ozone rumble of a patient, plodding streetcar; a Friday po-boy and beer at Parkway Bakery or the College Inn; red and purple houses, fuchsia and mango houses; the Saints and their delicious seasonal anguish; the parades, meeting friends out on the route, waving and yelling as the colors played under the oaks; naming the smells and seasons of our flowers, settling in for a life under our long, soft light. It was almost impossible to believe it had ever been real, that lovely liar's lacework heaven; the merest glance at the mummied gray park around us shredded it utterly. Maybe that was the other half of what was funny: that we could live here, in this death, and still be alive.

WE ATE Marion's garlic bread with *The History of the Rosary* on TV in the next room.

"Why so quiet, Janet?" By which she meant that the usual cover-fire of chatter I threw over EWTN—to what I knew was her annoyance, although her manners would never let her admit it—was conspicuously missing, and that her religious programming proved more fragile in the face of silence than under direct harassment.

"I'm just hung over."

"Oh, Donnie's father used to get the worst hangovers," she sang, her face glazing at the chance to talk about one of the two dead men who dominated her inner life. My appetite sublimated and wisped away as Marion told off the familiar beads of her widowhood. Marion's terrible secret was that she was happier without her husband, but she affected a solemnity that demanded credit for her sufferings. I carried my plate to the counter. "One time we were at a party where all they had was white wine, and—Janet, where are you going?"

"I'm thinking maybe Houston."

But I never made it off the porch; the sight of the trailer at the curb sapped my strength, and I plopped to the steps.

"I just wonder whether I might be less icky somewhere else," I explained when Don caught up.

"Do I have to remind you of the what-we-learned-about-other-places-when-we-evacuated lesson? Do I have to remind you about Lake Village?"

"What the fuck is that?"

"That place in Arkansas." He could see me remembering a stretch of road with five Baptist churches and no bars. We'd seen a man punch a dog and then cry in apology.

"Who said anything about Lake Village? I said Houston."

Don repeated the choicest of the aspersions we'd assembled for Houston over the years: that it was a replicant hell of robot ambition, that I'd have to learn to wear makeup, that I'd have to pretend the whole Texas-thing wasn't a big joke. That there would be a lot of work in New Orleans for a real estate lawyer, useful work; and I could not realistically leave my mother anyway, who would be as immovable as a pyramid. Then he pulled a familiar gray box from his pocket.

"Oh, shit. Did you just grab that on the way out?"

"I keep it in that desk by the door," he said, kneeling and lifting its bivalve.

The ring inside, in its satin pinch, had settled into a vintage silence since he'd first sprung it on me at twenty-two. It had thrown me into a sort of deaf shock that first time, my ears boxed from within, and the other two times had been almost as bad—weeks of clashing cymbals in my head.

"With your pepper spray and loose change?"

It should be obvious by now that Don and I had evolved a way of speaking that employed the weapons of acerbity and indirection to land blows on the dull-eyed sacred cows of culture. But I had never felt the falseness of that way of speaking, the decades-long mummery of it, until he asked, simply, "When will it be time, Janet? What are you holding onto?"

He shut the box and sat down beside me. I looked at Don: his worn eyes sinking into the sands of his face, his shrubbed gray hair. Myself: petty, terminally contrary, always at least a little angry at everything I couldn't ignore. Whatever I had been holding onto, it was now lost.

AND SO I went outside the next morning to wait for Don on my porch. It was another of those amazing New Orleans days that make you remember the earth was here before people and will be here after us: bright and blushing, quietly fulfilling its promise to itself, breathing itself in in one long breath. But the quaint notion I had of waving to Don from my swing was foiled by the stench of the refrigerators. I'd thought I was being clever by binding my fridge with duct tape before moving it, having heard enough stories about what was inside to know I didn't want the door to come open; but the moment Don and I tipped it onto the hand truck, it pissed a virile brown stream through the seal, puddling the tile with a reek I can only compare to the waft of a high-summer garbage truck—the way the shock and awe of that smell acquaint the nose with terror. It took me two days of mopping and airing to unstink my kitchen, and until a crane truck came by to pick up the units in November, the only thing we could do about the fruit flies swarming the neighborhood was to set dishes of red wine on our counters and wait for the intemperate bugs to drown themselves by the dozen. My neighbor was one of many of people in the city who had labeled the contents of his discarded unit, with red spray paint, MICHAEL BROWN INSIDE.

My body felt floaty and fake by the time I answered Don's knock. I was wearing my green suit, the one most recently tailored and most successful in its bid to make something attractive of my hair and skin. Don, whose best clothes were whatever I bought him every two years at Stein Mart, was wearing khaki pants and a white shirt, both incompletely ironed, a tie with yellow birds that I had complimented once ten years earlier, and a linen jacket of faded split-pea. Above the cinched collar his head looked gigantic and proud of itself. He produced a corsage from behind his back. I used his wrist to pull him inside.

When he saw me retouching my mascara in the kitchen, he exhaled onto the sofa and started fanning himself with a magazine.

"Finish your grading?" I asked.

"About half of it. There's only so much you can take in one sitting."

"In this paper I will talk about three ways Jesus helped me after the storm."

"Way one is He was always there for me."

"Way two is we found a gas station right before we ran out of gas."

"Way three is quit foofing around and let's go." He jangled his watch to read it. "I thought you told Billy we'd be there for ten."

Billy was a law-school friend and a man whose three sons Don had taught, now a judge in traffic court.

"You obviously don't know the first thing about judges. Anyway, we've got to take this trailer back before we go downtown."

We popped across the bridge and GPS'd our way through the terrible foreign land on the other side.

The kid behind the warehouse desk looked exactly as I'd pictured him, remediated teeth, scalp showing through shellacked hair, a T-shirt that said STOP STARING AT MY TITS.

"Y'all don't look like people who would steal things."

"Can you unhitch it? We're kind of dressed up."

Out in the yard, amid the bustle of stage properties floating to and fro in the morning sun, the kid disengaged the trailer, and I wrote a check. But when I held it out, he waved it off.

"I just rolled it into their budget. You'd shit if you saw the money these people have. I pick my *nose* while this movie is in town, I charge them for a box of Kleenex."

A zephyr of fellow feeling blew up inside me.

"Your house did OK?"

"Naw," he said cheerily. "We live in Chalmette. Twelve feet. We're on cots in the back of the warehouse, waiting for a trailer."

The next day Don hung the first of his paintings in my living room—*Seth Begat Enos,* an oil portrait of a rabbit—and I told people at the office that I had a new last name. I couldn't have upset them more if I had shown up topless or announced that I had accepted Satan as my personal savior. The senior partner shook my hand with a pained smile that suggested he would rather pay for my annulment than suffer the discomfort of speaking my new name, which to this day comes out of his mouth as unnaturally as *cocksucker* would come out of Marion's. Aside from the pedestrian hassles of reprinting stationery and replacing the gold letters on the entryway wall, I think it's as simple as that they had always known me in one way—as Janet Mehlhorn—and I was making them know me in another. Change offends the senses. And there's so much offense here that the heart and mind can't compass it. So we squint out into the daylight and haggle with adjustors, we mask up and mold-bomb our gutted houses, we file injunctions against the City's property fiats. And at night we cling in the dark to Don Violet, Jesus Christ, the rooms where we once played. The whole holy lost past.